T.H.E.M.

T.H.E.M.

G. C. Edmondson

DOUBLEDAY & CO., INC.
GARDEN CITY, NEW YORK
1974

All of the characters in this book are fictitious,
and any resemblance to actual persons, living
or dead, is purely coincidental.

Library of Congress Cataloging in Publication Data

Edmondson, G. C.
T.H.E.M.

I.   Title.
PZ4.E2387Ch5   [PS3555.D6]
ISBN 0-385-02532-7
Library of Congress Catalog Card Number 73–10968
Copyright © 1974 by G. C. Edmondson
All Rights Reserved
Printed in the United States of America
First Edition

T.H.E.M.

CHAPTER ONE

Ahtt! AHTT! The sound reverberated through his subconscious. In Turkish it meant "horse." He came up through layers of sleep. There were no Turks aboard this ship.

"Ahtt! Ya Ahtt!"

Art sighed himself awake and triggered the intercom. "In my cabin." He paused and hopefully added, "Asleep." Sighing again, he zipped his jump suit. He was floating down the companionway when the shout came again. "Ahtt! Where you?"

Jorf was curled into a fetal ball over the holo when he reached the bridge. Apart from a Greek ordinary whose name Art couldn't remember there was nobody else. The Old Man let go of the holo. Wordlessly he pointed. Art looked. He shrugged. "Just about on time, aren't they?"

Jorf pointed again. The Friend-or-Foe was not flashing. Art aimed the stylus at the largest light on the screen. Nothing happened. He tried another. He swept the stylus back and forth, covering the couple of hundred pinpoints which drifted across the holo. He banged his fist against the FOF but it did not flash.

"T.H.E.M.," Jorf said.

Art felt a sudden crawling as his masculinity tried to retreat up his inguinal canals. How, he wondered, did a professional coward get into situations like this? "You sure?" he asked. The Old Man didn't bother to answer.

Art switched ranges. The lights moving across the holo congealed into one bright spot in its center. On one edge was the brighter glow of the sun. He fiddled with ranges and finally found the pip that was Earth. The FOF was still not flashing. The Old Man made swimming motions and elbowed him away. He ranged the far side of the sun and finally Art saw the Allies. There were, he guessed, as many as there were of T.H.E.M. This time the FOF was flashing.

The Allied fleet was a light hour away, swinging a wild orbit to slingshot off the sun and whatever planets happened to be handy. Art looked at Jorf.

"About the same time," Jorf said to his unspoken question. "We going have grandstand seat."

"Should we warn them?"

"They got better equipment."

"So what do we do?"

"Sit, watch."

Art glanced nervously at him. "Want me to say anything?" In the background the two-toned high-low beeps of T.H.E.M. radio stuttered.

Jorf shook his graying bullet head. "Got maybe twenty hours. Go sleep."

Art nodded and pushed off toward the shaft. Drifting back to his own cubicle he knew he would not sleep. He wondered if the Old Man would. Jorf was used to changing plans. What worried Art was that the Old Man was not used to sitting and watching. He consoled himself with the knowledge that the *Nishrub* was not a combat ship.

Earth had been consoling itself in numerous ways lately, most people thanking their gods that the alien ambassador had arrived in time. If T.H.E.M. had come without warning, President Nixon might have gone down in history as the man who lost the first real World War. For this was not some internal convulsion. It was Earth *vs.* T.H.E.M. And thanks to a friendly warning, Earth stood a fair chance.

The Alliance had had to work fast. But each national propaganda machine had dutifully ground out the ambassador's statements with appropriate local slant and color.

A year ago Art had been a draft dodger, snorkeling about the polluted Mediterranean waiting for Nixon to die or Vietnam to declare another dividend. Then one day some astronomer had been fiddling with a comparator, flashing plates back and forth, when he noticed the telltale shift that meant a comet. Before he could get this not very exciting news to the wire services another observatory reported a luminous object the size of a small planet heading in from beyond Pluto. Its course threatened to coincide with Earth's.

Hot lines became busy. Church attendance improved. Small

African nations protested it was all a gigantic plot, but before anyone could push the button it became obvious that if the Whatever kept losing speed at the same rate it would be standing still by the time it reached Earth. Suddenly the button pushers realized they might all end up on the same side.

Before any new draft calls could be issued, several missile tracking stations had more disquieting news. Though the planetoid-sized thing still out beyond Jupiter was decelerating to match Earth's orbital speed, something was not. Hours later lenses resolved that something else into a hundred-meter-long torpedo heading straight for Earth.

The US of A's Apollo program had terminated and there was nothing on the launching pads. A half hour's frantic teletyping over the hot line proved only that, though the Soviet Union had a Soyuz thruster ready, not even the most openhanded offers of assistance could get it off in time to intercept the Earthbound missile. While commentators speculated and waited for the next missile from the decelerating invader, Art Jansen, sitting in a dank bar on a rainy afternoon in Marbella, wondered if perhaps one might not be enough.

It was confusing though. Like any young man, Art knew such arcane terms as hyperspace and ion drives. The invaders were using neither. Their ship was decelerating with rockets. Observers detected traces of radioactivity but the prime-time panel shows all conjectured: Was the water vapor from hypergolic fuel, or was water being used as reaction mass for a nuclear drive? When the experts were through analyzing, it turned out nobody knew. Meanwhile the missile was drawing closer.

Then tracking stations reported a slight change in course. The missile was going to pass by, barely skimming Earth's atmosphere a hundred miles up. Surplus stores reported a run on gas masks. Hours later people learned the missile's real purpose when it began broadcasting, droning its message of greetings in every known Earth language, plus a couple which scholars later learned had been inadvertently left over from the last program.

So great was the joy and relief that a few sorehead anthropologists who tried to remind people what happens when a superior technology contacts an inferior were told to stuff it up their Royal Hawaiians or they'd be given back to the Indians. Experts with less qualification rhapsodized about Coming of Age and being admitted into the galaxywide Brotherhood of Man. Others, extrapolating from scale counts in Japanese monster movies thought a Brotherhood of Eclectic Malthusians more fitting to the actuality. By the time somebody broke that down to its initials the missile was orbiting in for a soft landing.

Since all this happened in less than a week, Art Jansen was still sitting in the same dank bar in Marbella, wondering what the ambassador would look like when he stepped out and if it would ever stop raining. His first question was answered when the TV began live coverage relayed over Spain's national network.

It seemed to be raining at Kennedy too where ordinary traffic had been rerouted until further notice. Art clung to his bar stool and resisted all efforts by latecomers to sit in his lap. The hundred-meter missile came in on its fiery tail. A boarding ramp was hurriedly run out but even from Marbella Art could see it was going to be far short of reaching. The hatch halfway up the side opened and the ambassador posed momentarily, looking rather ordinary except for his oddly tailored jump suit.

There was a collective gasp as he stepped into thin air. Then when everyone realized he was not going to spread any wings the commentators tried to describe his flying belt. Since his belt was invisible these descriptions bordered on the fanciful. Watching over Spain's black-and-white-only network, Art wondered if their descriptions of the ambassador's hair color were equally fanciful.

Thinking about it after all these months, Art no longer wondered what the Alliance ambassador would do. What kept him awake was what the Old Man might do. He had known Jorf longer than the Alliance had existed. Art didn't know which frightened him the most.

He wriggled free of the sleeping harness. Drifting toward the bridge he wished he'd done something prudent like volunteering for hazardous duty in Vietnam. There at least, he would never have met Jorf.

The Old Man still clung to the holo when Art entered the bridge. The Greek ordinary had been relieved by an aging blue-eyed man who spoke bad French and worse Arabic while stoutly maintaining that he could not understand German. The blue-eyed man glanced at

Jorf's back and shook his head. Art ignored the warning and drifted around where Jorf could see him.

"*Allah akhbar,*" Jorf muttered and glanced up.

"Since when are you getting religion?" Art asked.

Jorf had punched some new instructions into the holo. Now the Allied fleet was a mass of islamic green pinpoints near the upper right. T.H.E.M.s glowed in a red sickle near the center. Art circled the holo image and saw the sickle was actually a shallow bowl shape drifting nearly motionless in the path of the advancing Allies. Each of the red pinpricks bore the fuzzy outlines of ionization. Art realized they were retro firing, trying to get some way on in the opposite direction so the Allied fleet would not pass through and out of range in a micro-second. Though the fleets were on collision courses the chances of ships colliding or even seeing each other were microscopic, stationed as they were at five-thousand-kilometer intervals.

"How much longer?" Art asked.

Jorf squinted and ran a hand over the gray millimeter-long stubble on his scalp. "Allies not slowing down," he said. "Damn soon."

It didn't make sense. The Allied fleet could easily pass unscathed through T.H.E.M. but the point was to destroy the enemy, not to leave him unharmed between the fleet and home. "What do you suppose went wrong?" Art asked.

Jorf shrugged, leaving him to wonder if there was some secret plan. Perhaps they and the *Nishrub* were an unknowing part of it.

According to orders, the *Nishrub* had cleared Earth orbit two months ago and blasted her leisurely way out to the asteroids for artesian water. *Artesian* because asteroidal ice would not consume megaton-days of thrust to draw it from the bottom of some planetary gravity well.

Art remembered the prime-time panel shows back when Earth had first spotted the Allied contact ship. One of their guesses had been right. The Allies dropped out of hyperspace as near a solar system as DED reckoning could put them and covered the remaining light hours or days, depending on the navigator's intuition, with nuclear rockets. The *Nishrub*'s job was like an oiler's in naval warfare on Earth. Slow and unarmed, the tanker put out ahead of the fleet to scrounge for artesian water, which, in the asteroid belt, meant kilometer diameter blocks of ice which could be wrapped in black solar absorptive envelopes and vacuum distilled into the waterboat's hull for chemically pure reaction mass.

They had expected to finish prospecting for water a month from now, then take another three for the slow run out past Pluto where the Allied fleet was to refuel and deploy. Now T.H.E.M. were already inside the asteroids, within easy distance of Earth, and the Allied fleet had so much way on that it promised to pass ineffectually through T.H.E.M.

The Greek ordinary whose name Art still couldn't remember drifted into the bridge and relieved the blue-eyed man on watch. Art hung around for a futile moment, wanting to ask questions and knowing there were no answers. Finally he pushed off down the shaft again. The blue-eyed man was waiting. *"Qu'est ce que sera de nous?"* he asked in his barbarous accent.

"How should I know what's going to happen to us?" Art replied.

"But . . . he tells you things."

"Some things and some times."

"But you must know something."

"I know we're in for trouble. Better sleep while you can."

The blue-eyed man growled in guttural French and drifted up the shaft.

"AHTT!"

Art hastened back to the bridge. The Old Man still clung to the holo, squinting from various angles as he tried to understand what the Allied fleet was up to. "Crazy," he growled. "Already we losing."

Art mumbled something conciliatory.

"How much we got?" Jorf added.

Knowing that Jorf would know better than himself how many of the *Nishrub*'s five tanks were loaded, Art was careful. "One to four are full," he said. "Last time I was on watch you were just starting to fill five."

"What temperature?"

Art studied dials. Normally cargo was carried at 4° Centigrade, which gave maximum density and still left the mass liquid for easy transfer. "Everything normal," he said. "Stuff in No. Five's a half-degree warmer since it's still trickling in from the still." Trickling was a relative term since the hunk of slush and glacial rock alongside was pouring several thousand gallons per hour into the tanker.

"Turn off heat," Jorf said.

"But the tanks'll freeze!"

"Cut all power and maybe we disappear."

Art wondered if the Old Man was finally growing cautious. Normally this far in the *Nishrub* would keep its tanks warm by placing its black side to the sun. But the crew had spent days finicking about with portable attitude stabilizers to take the spin out of this orbiting mass of rock and ice. Only then had they been able to set up the miles-wide black blister. For the still to work the *Nishrub*'s waiting tanks had to be cold, so the tanker lay in the shadow of the ice it was melting.

Art wondered whether cutting power would render them invisible. Surely T.H.E.M. radar could detect mass but . . . The *Nishrub* was only eight hundred meters long. Perhaps without power she would register as another small asteroid. These rocks could be anything from solid ice to solid metal, depending on what part of the shattered ur-planet they came from. But meanwhile, they would sit here quietly and hope T.H.E.M. did not see them. There was a chance, Art guessed, unless they had the million-to-one bad luck of a visual sighting.

"Go outside," Jorf said. "Tell everybody fold it."

Art was about to ask why he couldn't do it over the radio when he realized the Old Man was a long jump ahead as usual. He wondered how sensitive T.H.E.M. radio was. He was pushing off to suit up when he remembered to ask, "How close is the nearest?"

"Too damn close," Jorf muttered. "Allied commander crazy."

Art went to his cubicle and suited up. Apart from magnetic shoes the suit was almost like the diving gear he had learned to use in the Mediterranean once he had graduated from snorkels and started playing for keeps with coast guards. Going through the airlock he could hear the occasional grunt and murmur as men worked at keeping the blister watertight, padding protrustions, using alpenstocks to knock off jagged rocks. Some idiot was cluttering up the band with an obscene song in Urdu, punctuated by grunts as he struggled to stretch the blister over a greater expanse of rock and ice.

Art wanted to yell at them all to shut up but Jorf could have done that from inside. He gripped his alpenstock and went through the low pressure lock. It was dark inside the still and faintly warmer. He kicked off and drifted toward the nearest light.

The man looked up and stared in puzzlement while Art reached over and flipped off his radio. Art put his faceplate against the other's and talked diver-fashion. Finally the other understood his tinny shouts and nodded. Art moved to the next light.

It took nearly an hour to contact everyone but finally they followed him through the lock into sunlight. Somewhere the endless obscene song was still spilling into an open mike. Art wondered, if T.H.E.M. could hear it. Surely the Old Man could.

Outside men patrolled the blister, stretching it as the ice melted and entrapped rocks came adrift to nuzzle each other in the almost zero gravity. Art saw two men near the airlock but the rest were hidden by the rock's curvature. As the last Inside man came through the airlock he took the slate from his kangaroo pocket and printed RADIO SILENCE. ROLL UP.

But if they started the blister would lose pressure, bringing all kinds of startled questions from the Outside crew. He lettered TELL OUTSIDE FIRST and pantomimed until each man had copied the message on his own slate. Art hooked his alpenstock in the ice and swung toward an Outside man. He drifted off and had to fire a gram-second to get back down.

Waiting to settle, he squinted at the shrunken sun, which glittered like a welder's arc. Somewhere out there two fleets would meet. He wondered if the *Nishrub* would actually be able to see a tiny distant flash as some fighting ship ceased to exist. Nobody on Earth had ever actually seen a T.H.E.M. ship. He hoped they wouldn't be too superior to the ships the Alliance had hastily trained Earth crews to man. Art had never seen an Alliance fighting ship either.

Not that there was anything wrong with the tanker . . . the *Nishrub* worked as well as ever, he guessed, but paint could not disguise long hard use.

From this height Art could see all of the black, heat-absorbing blister. Half of the Outside men had been warned. Grunts and muffled curses came from the men who still struggled to extend the blister over the shrinking ball of rock and ice. That endless obscene song was still adorning the air waves.

Art hit the surface with a gentle bump and crawled around until the next man could see his slate. The face inside the suit was cheerful to the point of idiocy. It nodded and went back to work. Art pointed at his slate. The man waved and smiled back. His lips never stopped moving. Art moved closer and unplugged the man's mike. The obscene lyrics abruptly ceased. He put his faceplate against the other's and shouted. Finally the other man's face lit in understanding.

Art kicked off high enough to see the whole blister again. As a boy he had dreamed of floating in space, exposed to the naked glory of the stars. Compared to skin diving, it was uneventful. There were no sharks or moray eels or inquisitive barracuda in space. He gave a wry grin and reflected that if he'd started out in space instead of snorkeling about in that open sewer they called the Mediterranean his life line would never have become tangled with Jorf's.

They were tearing loose the seal along the far edge. He popped off a gram-second and started back down to help, then wondered if Jorf would want him inside. To hell with the Old Man, he decided. For a few minutes he could stay out of range of Jorf's shouts and indulge in the satisfaction of some hard physical exercise. But one seldom forgets the person who saves his life. He wondered if Jorf even remembered.

Art sighed. Though it sounds like the title of some mighty thewed Martian from the days before everyone knew there weren't any, Jorf is a common name in some parts of Earth. But this Jorf was an uncommon man. Art bumped the surface and hooked his way toward the men rolling the blister.

Working in the sunlight over rocks slightly warmed by the black envelope, Art felt a trickle of sweat. Staring ahead where the hose led to the ship hidden on the shadowy side, he was startled by a reddish flash. Another red pinpoint shot up and he realized the Old Man was firing signals.

He kicked off. When he was high enough to see the dim outlines of the *Nishrub* he took aim and fired a gram-sec burn. Then he realized the Old Man might be in a hurry. "Last of the big spenders," he muttered, and fired another five gram-secs.

Jorf still hunched over the holo when he re-entered the bridge. "You wanted me?" Art asked.

"How long to finish?"

"Maybe two hours. Are we going somewhere?"

Jorf didn't answer.

Art tried to read his back. "You fired some rockets," he hinted.

Jorf pulled himself around to study the holo from another direction. After several seconds he grunted, "Yeah?"

"If you don't need me here I'll go help fold up."

"Better you stay."

There were times when Art suspected the Old Man liked him. But it was hard to tell. He began climbing out of his life suit. Suddenly Jorf gave another grunt.

"Something happen?"

"First kill."

"T.H.E.M. or us?"

"Us."

Art wondered if Jorf believed in omens. The Old Man was sharper than a pocketful of razor blades but sometimes there seemed to be odd bits of Harún er Rashíd rattling around in his head. "You think we're going to win?" Art asked.

Jorf looked up. "Radios off?" he asked.

"Radio silence complete."

Jorf checked switches on the bridge mikes. "Why Jews win Arabs?" he asked.

Art thought a moment and suddenly realized every Arab he had ever known had been a brave fighter. "I guess they're trained in modern technology and know their weapons better," he guessed. He looked into the holo. Two more lights flared briefly and disappeared. Both had been green. "I suppose T.H.E.M. crews have been with their ships a long time," Art said unhappily. "What do you suppose'll happen if we lose?"

"You saw pictures of last planet," Jorf said.

Another green light flared out. Art circled the holo. T.H.E.M. ships were still in a shallow bowl, like a catcher's mitt. The Alliance had lost speed so rapidly that Art realized he had not been told the whole truth about a fighting ship's capabilities. He wondered how men could do anything under such severe G-stress. He guessed they must've preprogrammed the battle before climbing into G-hammocks. And now several thousand men had just died in hammocks, their ships blown up before the two fleets were even properly in range.

The holo flared again, this time lighting the whole bridge with a green glow. Then half of the Alliance fleet was missing.

Art did mental arithmetic. A hundred ships at five thousand men per ship . . . it was too much to grasp. "Damn the Alliance!" he murmured. But it wasn't the Alliance's fault. T.H.E.M. would have invaded Earth anyway. This way Earth could go down fighting. He studied the holo. They were getting in range now. He watched red T.H.E.M. lights, waiting for one to flare and go out. Five more green lights flared into oblivion.

Art was afraid he was going to vomit. He took a deep breath. Jorf glanced at him and back to the holo. The Old Man's expressionless, hooded gaze had always haunted Art with some childhood memory he could never quite dredge up. He tried to remember, to get his mind off what was happening. A half million Earthmen had just died. Probably he had known some of them. He wondered what would happen to Earth.

The Old Man switched ranges. The shallow bowl formation of T.H.E.M. still had the fuzzy ionization outlines of deceleration. Though "advancing" like bullets in passing gear, relative motion made them stand practically still for the *Nishrub*. Within an hour the tanker would be engulfed by the tenuous dish. Art wondered if T.H.E.M. would bother with anything this small. He remembered vaguely the conventions of Nelson's day when a ship of the line would not lower its dignity by sinking a frigate. Did T.H.E.M. observe any rules of warfare? He remembered films the alien ambassador had shown on one T.H.E.M. pacified planet.

He studied the holo's ranging scale. T.H.E.M. would pass beyond the *Nishrub* before they could reverse direction. Then they would pass back the same way as they pursued the Allies. Art guessed the nearest would pass within a couple of hundred thousand kilometers, half the distance from Earth to Moon. He hoped their ain't-nobody-here-but-us-chickens tactic would be successful. But how long could the *Nishrub* hold out? Fuel and water were no problem but their food would not last forever.

The remainder of the Allied fleet was entering the dish now. Perhaps they would get through. But now they were outnumbered two to one and had not yet damaged a single T.H.E.M. Another green light flared and disappeared.

Jorf glanced at the chronometer. Only five minutes had passed since Art had come in. "To hell with still," the Old Man said. "Tell everybody come in."

Art nodded and floated into the airlock. He was closing the last zipper on his suit when he heard the hiss of cycling air. The outer door opened and he kicked off from the faint pull of ship and rock. Finally he was high enough to see the wrinkled blister on the opposite side. He fired and began tacking downgrav. The crew stretched along a two-kilometer line fighting to roll the still and fold it down to a manageable size. The micron-thick black plastic weighed next to nothing but here the men also weighed nothing and it was slow, awkward work as they squirmed for purchase against the ice, spinning off and scrabbling with alpenstocks for some kind of a grip. Art touched down and put his faceplate against the man's at one end of the line.

From somewhere came the steady rasp of breathing and he realized somebody's mike was on again. Oh well, the ship's repeater was turned off. Life suit radios would not carry fifty kilometers even under perfect line-of-sight conditions. Unless T.H.E.M. had better detectors than . . . Remembering what happened to the Allied fleet, Art realized T.H.E.M. must have several tricks Earthmen had not been warned about. He wondered if the other off-Earth races had known about them.

Alliance crews came from half a thousand inhabitable systems in that corner of the galaxy. Art had seen films of home life on some planets and watched interviews of the training officers sent to Earth. What held the Alliance together, as Art saw it, was the absolute and uncompromising brutality of T.H.E.M. He remembered a history professor explaining how the United States and Russia had declared eternal friendship after taking a long look at Hitler.

He tried to ignore the breathing that was coming over the life suit radio. The Old Man would want to know if everyone was safe aboard. He started counting the specks a half kilometer below. He could feel the warmth of the distant sun on his back. He tried to shake the sweat off his brow but it ran down in his eyes. That was one problem he had never had working the Mediterranean in a wet suit.

He had counted fifty-eight men when he was filled with a sudden chill horror. He remembered a day in the Med when the watery sunlight had been abruptly blotted out. Looking up, he had seen a twenty-foot-long shark glide leisurely overhead. But there were no sharks in the asteroid belt. Art twisted his neck to see what was blocking off the sun.

The whole hemisphere of sky behind him was dark. Art remembered how erratic were the orbits of these city-sized rock fragments. But the *Nishrub*'s ranging computer was supposed to scan everything close by and predict this kind of near miss. He squinted into the darkness trying to guess the size and relative speed. Distances were deceptive in space. The shadow might be ten kilometers away and it might be a thousand. He waited a minute for his glare shield to clear. Gradually his eyes adjusted to the darkness. He saw that the planetoid's surface was smoother than the usual jagged rocks. Then Art felt the sweat on his face turn abruptly colder. This was not an asteroid drifting by. It was a T.H.E.M. ship.

CHAPTER TWO

For an instant Art was totally paralyzed. Not even during Jorf's wilder moments in the Mediterranean had Art felt this total mind-boggling terror. He could see nearly invisible cracks around openings on the side of the ship now, and alien squiggles which were probably numbers.

Abruptly he saw he was moving closer. Good God, he thought, it must be a hundred miles long! The ship had overcome the slight pull of the rock and he was falling toward it. He would be captured and drift along like a miniature moon, orbiting T.H.EM. long after his air was used up. If he fired his thruster to get away, would T.H.E.M. notice? What was the ship doing here anyway if it had not already scented the *Nishrub?* He pointed his thruster and held the trigger for what seemed an eternity before the black immensity began to recede. Holding his breath, he waited for retribution. Still echoing in his helmet was the sound of breathing. If they were both alive ten minutes from now he resolved to kill that breather.

Drifting back toward the rock, he saw the crew hooking their frantic way toward the airlock. Several had already passed through. Behind, the sunward half of the universe was still blotted out by the T.H.E.M. ship. It seemed to creep along no faster than cars on the Seville toll road.

Art released pent-up breath. He was still alive. By now Jorf would be shrieking polylingual blasphemies wondering where he was. Perhaps he ought to crowd in through the airlock ahead of the waiting crew. It would be the logical thing, for Jorf would need him soon. But it was so much what he wanted to do that Art suspected he'd better not.

There were still eighty men outside and the airlock could only hold eight at a time. He glanced at his watch. Thirty seconds to crowd in, fifteen to cycle, another thirty to get through the inside door. . . . What am I worrying about, he wondered? If they saw us, we're dead already. Still, he knew death would be more acceptable inside the ship, close to the rest of the dying. And if what the Allies said about T.H.E.M. was true, it was better to die.

The door beneath him opened and eight more men crowded in. Suddenly Art caught a glint of motion on the far side of the half-rolled blister. He squinted and wished he had one of the better suits with built-in binoculars and radar. At the edge of his vision he caught the hint of movement again. Now what the hell? He glanced behind. T.H.E.M. still covered half the sky, its edges blurred in the distance.

Thanks to its shadow he could not make out what was moving down on the blister. Probably water vapor trying to escape and the blister was flapping. But in the shadow there would be no vapor. He pointed his thruster and landed by a suited crewman still trying to roll up the blister.

The same cretin face gave him a smile. Art groaned. The man's mike was plugged in again. Art pulled it out and the hoarse breathing stopped. Remembering the last time he'd shouted and gesticulated, he jerked a peremptory thumb and hooked the man's alpenstock with his own. Moonface gave a delighted grin as they floated high enough to blast back down toward the airlock. Glancing at the happy face behind him, Art tried to remember which of the German immortals had said, "Against stupidity even the gods strive in vain." He pushed the breather ahead into the mass of waiting men.

The sky in the direction the T.H.E.M. ship was still gliding from turned brighter. A minute passed and he knew he was seeing the end. Close as he was, it was hard to visualize the whole ship, but he supposed it was the same round-ended capsule as every other ship he had seen. No flames were coming from this end so it had to be retro firing. How long, he wondered, would it take for this large a ship to stop and reverse direction. The markings on the sides didn't seem to be moving any slower.

Finally there were only five men waiting. Art thrust down to the surface. To his disgust, one was Moonface. He made sure Moonface went in first. Moments later he unzipped his mask and began breathing ship air.

Jorf was watching the holo. "You see it?" he asked.

"I saw it. How far away is it?"

"Twelve kilometers to this edge."

Art shuddered. "You think they know we're here?"

Jorf shrugged and rubbed a hand over his gray, millimeter-long hair. "We lose," he said.

Art wondered how the Old Man could take it so calmly. There was a bright red light near the holo's center which he supposed was the ship outside. Around the *Nishrub,* still in their unbroken bowl formation, hovered the T.H.E.M. fleet. Here and there green lights showed the scattered Allies trying to escape. As he watched another flared out.

"Now what?" Art asked.

There was a look about Jorf—a look Art dreaded from Mediterranean days. But all the Old Man said was, "Muster. Everybody come in?"

"I hope so." Art punched the PA and shouted "Muster aft," in as many languages as he could remember.

There were anguished remarks from those who had been off duty and sleeping but finally muster was over and to Art's faint surprise all two hundred were there.

Jorf thought a moment, considering how to break the news. "War's over," he finally said. "We lose." He returned to the bridge, leaving Art to interpret.

"What the hell he mean, we lose?" somebody shouted in almost English.

By the time Art had repeated the news in enough languages almost an hour had passed. After their initial disbelief the crew seemed numbed. Art guessed he would be too if he ever got time to think about it.

Earth was finished. There were habitable planets somewhere in the galaxy but he didn't know where. Even if they could find one, the *Nishrub*'s crew were all men. He decided to get the supply officer off to one side and find out how long they could eat. *God damn it!* he thought, *We were such an unimportant little planet. Why couldn't we have gone on killing one another in our quaint, old-fashioned ways?*

But the ambassador had pointed out that it was too late for that. T.H.E.M. were already coming to end Earth's isolation more abruptly than Perry had ended Japan's.

The sun had finally come out on the Costa del Sol but Art was still in the same Marbella bar when the ambassador had come live from New York, dubbed into language which most Spaniards address only to their saints. Listening to platitudes about galactic unity, Art learned the Alliance races all looked human. The next significant word was T.H.E.M.

Alliance Intelligence had not garnered much information about T.H.E.M. The *T*heriomorph *H*ellbent *E*nemy *M*ission had appeared one day from the endless unexplored reaches of the galaxy. Until then the Alliance had traded with each other, occasionally engaging in a bit of sharp practice, but never believing that warfare between stars could be practical.

While THEM scorched planet after planet the Alliance had tried every known means of signaling. THEM answered no signals. THEM accepted no surrender. THEM ships self-destructed when they were losing. From odd-shaped debris the Alliance concluded THEM were not human. No one knew what they looked like, or anything except that they *could* be stopped.

Their ships were so similar to Alliance ships that one theory held they were a race of planetbound primitives who had captured an exploring Alliance trader and taken it from there.

The ambassador thought Earth might have ten months. Even a properly tooled-up yard took something over six Earth years to build a ship. The Alliance was overextended, fighting for survival. They could lend a few officers for training Earth to run the ships they could furnish. No, they weren't totally obsolete. But they weren't the latest thing off the drawing boards either. If Earth buckled down and learned to operate the Alliance ships there was—just barely—a chance.

For once the US of A, the Soviet Union, and the People's Republic of China were in unanimous agreement: Small Emerging Nations could either shut up about violated sovereignty or they could go screw. In either event, all the aid programs' personnel and money were coming home where they could do some good. If any citizens of small African countries wished to enlist in the Alliance a well-armed recruiting party would stop at each village.

There was but one point the ambassador insisted upon. The Alliance would accept no unwilling fighters. There were no other restrictions. Any person, any age, any sex, any physical condition would be welcomed into the armed forces—but only if he or she wanted to put his whole heart and soul into defending Earth.

While left-wingers pointed out that world peace could have been achieved generations ago if every army had drafted the old, the deferrable, and the affluent, others were at pains to explain that in modern warfare physique was not as important as it had been in the infantry. Militant women's lib groups were frantically backpedaling.

Suspicious newsmen wondered why recruiting parties had to be armed if only volunteers were wanted. It turned out that the armed guards were to make sure local governments did not withhold volunteers or use the recruiters to empty local jails.

All of which was a violation of sovereignty. Politicians instinctively reacted against legislating themselves out of existence. But for once the will of the people was not to be thwarted. Those who obstructed found life dangerous. Within days the Alliance ambassador was *de facto* ruler of Earth. The ambassador insisted this was temporary, that once the threat of invasion was stemmed he would move on and Earthmen would once more be free to kill each other in the old familiar ways.

Some of the first unemployed were customs and immigration men from Earth's hundred forty-five countries. Sitting in that bar in Marbella, Art gloomily surveyed this blow to his own likelihood. He finished his beer and went back to the boat.

Jorf was down in the engine room fiddling with a demand regulator when he got there. "Allo, Ahtt," he said. "Ready go back tonight?"

Art told him about the ambassador's new edict.

Sitting cross-legged on a workbench, wrapped in a *djellaba*, old Jorf was a picture from a social studies text. *"Inshallah,"* he shrugged, then spoiled the effect by adding, "Staman bull gonna ruin business!"

Art was inclined to agree. Though he had often repented ever getting into the business, the money was good, the hours short, and he didn't know how he would ever again have it so good unless Nixon and Vietnam disappeared.

"You want *kif?*" the Old Man asked.

Art shook his head. "I want to keep my head on straight."

Jorf shrugged and lit his hand-rolled joint. "What you say true, we still go Africa tonight."

"Oh?"

"Only we don't come back."

Art sighed. It was slightly warmer down there and some places a hamburger tasted almost American. "But what'll we do for money?" he asked. "Go back to fishing?"

Jorf pulled deeply on his joint and didn't answer. When Art wandered back up to the bar the TV was showing *before* and *after* pictures. After THEM had moved on the whole planet looked like ground zero at Hiroshima. Art frowned and walked out into the street again. Wandering between the high-rise buildings, he looked in vain among the Swedish *flasköl* signs and countless German bars all called Onckel Willis for some evidence that he was in Spain. Finally down by the bookstore he heard a Spanish voice where men were emptying shelves and packing books in cartons. A Hanomag truck arrived and began unloading office furniture. "*¿Qué pasa?*" he asked the driver.

"Recruiting station," the man grunted, and continued wrestling with a file cabinet. Art went back to the bar.

"My own planet," the ambassador was saying, "is a cool green place very like yours. True, we have starships and a Faster Than Light drive. This war could be conducted more successfully if we could also devise a FTL radio but . . ." He shrugged. "In many respects Earth technology is equal, even superior to our own. There will be a demand for your miniaturized electronics once this war ends. Other planets in our Alliance have surpassed my own in medicine. Soon Earth's citizens may be happy and productive in their second century of life. Then there is food. Naturally no planet imports the easily synthesized basics but I have tasted Earth foods. Your bread is delicious."

Art shifted his mind out of gear and waited for the old bastard to get back to THEM. Instead, the ambassador took a break and there began an indoctrination film for would-be warriors aboard an Alliance ship.

Art was disappointed. He had expected way-out science. The Alliance seemed no more than twenty years beyond Earth, except for their balky and unpredictable FTL drive, which relied on dead reckoning and often required weeks of rocketry for a final landfall.

He had expected heat rays and the whole smegeggy of Buck

Rogerish invention, but Alliance ships had no shields apart from their metal hulls. Offensive armament was limited to armor-piercing nuclear warheads on chemical rockets. Listening to the droning description of heat and mass sensors, he realized some of the new laser-guided stuff in Vietnam would be more accurate than the Alliance's clumsy devices. He wondered if there would be time to install them in Alliance ships.

The stagnation of THEM technology on the same level as the Alliance's tended to reinforce the theory that they had possessed none of their own until they had somehow captured an Alliance ship. Once taken, its charts had furnished a ready-made invasion plan for the Alliance planets.

The Alliance wasn't making that mistake again. Location of the home planets was restricted information. This struck Art as the wrong time to lock the barn door but he supposed a lot of trouble could have been avoided if somebody had thought of it in time. Now THEM were making up in single-minded ferocity whatever they lacked in originality.

Meanwhile general staffs and admiralties had recovered from their initial shock. They began digging in for the protracted infighting that would resolve which way the gravy train would chug and who would end up Supreme Commander of Earth Forces. Each country had lengthy precedents and sound reasons for pressing its claim. The Soviet Union and the United States tacitly assumed that once the smaller nations had shouted themselves hoarse it would be a contest between the only two countries who had put men in space.

Then the ambassador dropped another blockbuster. When the armies, navies, and air forces stopped jockeying for position long enough to realize none of them were in the running, their screams of outrage were being drowned by the common man's belly laugh. The Alliance had its own tests for placement. Everyone enlisted as Lowest of the Low, with no guarantee of preference.

Experienced warriors knew this was so much democratic window dressing. Several American generals and a Soviet field marshal enlisted, expecting rapid promotion in the new command's power vacuum. When the Allied fleet was heading for its first engagement months later the field marshal was still chipping paint. He could have resigned any time he wanted but return to the Soviet Union after distinguishing himself thusly seemed even less attractive than chipping paint.

Two American generals commanded typewriters aboard an Alliance ship and the youngest admiral in the Navy was now a junior navigator aboard what the ambassador insisted on calling a corvette.

More interesting was the number of ship captains from places nobody had ever heard of. Many had atrocious table manners and depended on their aides for report writing and signing their names. The prime-time panel shows spent hours analyzing Alliance aptitude tests.

The passed-over thought it was all a vile Communist plot but the Soviet Union field marshal knew this explanation was inherently defective. What galled both industrial giants was Chinese on the HQ staff. Even the Japanese member was politely mystified.

Some commanders of Alliance ships had reasonable IQs. Others bordered on stupid. Arabs and Jews commanded. Someone complained that no Americans commanded. Someone said the same about the British, the Germans, and the Scandinavians. None of these accusations was true.

At the beginning there had been some effort to man ships by nationality or at least by linguistic group. But in the frenzy of manning an interstellar fleet in ten months even this had been dropped. Often a dozen nationalities were aboard the same ship, forced to communicate as best they could. These polyglot ships had a Talker, a man who could be profane and ungrammatical in a dozen languages.

Some South Africans and some South Mississippians complained about this rough and ready integration. Ship commanders told the complainers to resign and go home. But by now it was obvious that there were more volunteers than there were places. Most complainers stayed.

There had been complaints about food. Earthmen felt obliged to start the day with lactations evolved for the young of other species, or with herbal infusions of infinite variety. Occasionally these whims could be indulged. But fleet foodstuffs were synthesized aboard the larger ships and though it was technically feasible to duplicate Earth's hundred forty-five national cuisines, the time could better be spent manufacturing ammunition. Breakfast was a bland, dietetically balanced gruel seasoned with bitter memories. Art didn't like it. But then, he hadn't expected to like anything.

When he went back down to the dock Jorf was arguing with a *celador* in the Spanish customs. The trouble, Art supposed, would be the Spaniards' totally unreasonable attitude toward clearances. Probably this *celador* was insisting that the Old Man spend hours chasing from office to office getting the necessary stamps and signatures. In more enlightened countries customs men would spare shipowners this inconvenience in return for a small fee. Why, Art wondered, did the Spaniards have to carry honesty to such absurd lengths?

Finally the *celador* was gone. "You ready?" Jorf asked.

"I'm not going," Art said.

"What you mean, you not going?"

Art had been on the edge of a nervous breakdown since he had been aboard Jorf's boat. "There won't be any more money," he began.

Jorf brought to bear the seasoned philosophies of older, more mellow civilizations. With a gentle, tolerant smile he said, "Bullshit!"

"Sure, maybe someday things'll be supercolossal again," Art said. "But until this war's over you might as well forget it."

"You afraid?" Jorf asked.

Art thought a moment. "Not afraid," he said. "Unmanned, appalled, dismayed, perhaps petrified."

Jorf threw up his hands. "Always you make joke. I get you outa jail last time because you got seaman papers my ship. What the hell you gonna do?"

"I'll work something out. My nerves are shot. I need a rest."

"You need smoke *kif,* screw nice black girl."

"You may be right. I'll try it some day." Jorf was still shaking his head when Art swung up onto the dock. He was halfway to the bar when a *guardia civil* in black patent leather hat politely requested his presence at the *cuartel.*

He spent an hour in an anteroom while the *comandante* sifted through versions of whose parked car had perversely jumped into the middle of a cobbled street and damaged the municipality's donkey-drawn garbage truck. Finally a *guardia* beckoned him into the office. The *comandante* gazed long and mournfully at Art. Art waited in silence. The *comandante* lit a cigar and renewed his silent study. "You're out of a job," he finally said.

"A job?"

The *comandante* sighed. "Let us not waste time. You know what you have been doing. I know. We both know you will do it no longer. Soon you will run out of money and then it will be my pleasure to deport you back where your own government can do as it sees fit."

Art was silent for a moment. "You wouldn't be spelling this out unless there were an alternative," he guessed. "What do you want?"

The *comandante* smiled. "Some friends of mine need a diver who can be discreet."

Art thought over his chances of being alive when he had done whatever they wanted. He thought wistfully of Jorf. The Old Man was wild but he took care of his own. "My gear's aboard the boat," he said. "I'll have to get it if you want me to dive."

The *comandante* nodded. "I'll send some men."

"You'll send them a dozen times and meanwhile somebody will hide or toss overboard the vital part."

The *comandante* drew deeply on his cigar. Finally he nodded. "Two men will accompany you."

Art guessed that was the best he was going to do. He nodded and buttoned his jacket. Two *guardias* found their Napoleonic-vintage hats, buckled on their sidearms, and accompanied him.

"You guys got time to stop for a drink?" he asked. The *guardias* shook their heads. Art sighed and began walking toward the dock. Halfway there he noticed that the bookstore's conversion into recruiting center had been completed. Flanking the doorway were two gigantic blondish men in ill-fitting uniforms, each with a machine pistol slung over his shoulder. Walking between the pair of immaculately tailored *guardias civiles,* Art tried to guess what language the recruiting center guards would speak. They might even be American for all he knew. But if they had been posted to this country, chances were they would know Spanish.

"I am being restrained against my will!" he shouted. "I want to enlist in the Alliance forces." As the chunky blondish men hustled him through the door he heard the *guardias civiles* muttering. It sounded like the Spanish for shithead.

CHAPTER THREE

Art drifted back into the bridge. The red THEM lights still held formation. Art counted seven green lights still visible. The center of the holo was filled with the red glow of the ship he had seen outside. "How big is it?" he asked. "Same as the others?"

Jorf frowned. "Bigger maybe. What the hell it doing here?"

"This is the center of their formation."

"Why he don't kill us? We too small for big sonofabitch to bother?"

Art glanced worriedly at him. Jorf was a creature of moods. He remembered that afternoon in Marbella.

When Jorf had strode down the main street like some western shoot-out artist who had been led astray by the wardrobe department, the *guardia civil* had prudently decided it had wine and *tapas* to inspect on other streets. The Old Man's face had turned darker and his eyes— There was something about Jorf's eyes that Art had never understood. He had never been able to look into them long enough to be sure what color they were. Even here between blond soldiers in new, ill-fitting uniforms Art was frightened.

It wasn't that Jorf roared and threatened. But there was something not quite human about the Old Man's glance. Art had seen bulls die. He had tangled with sharks. Suddenly he knew what had always bothered him about Jorf. The Old Man's eyes flickered like an eagle's or a gamecock's.

It took half an hour but finally Art convinced him that he was not being shanghaied. He explained the squeeze that had been put upon him by the *guardia civil*.

"Balls!" Jorf growled. "You want come back, we go." He glared at the Alliance recruiter, who shrugged. "We take nobody who doesn't want to go," the recruiter said. "But you may have trouble with the local police."

"I take care of them," Jorf said.

Art visualized himself accompanying Jorf as the Old Man shot up *guardias civiles* on the way, then cut in his third, undeclared engine to outrun patrol boats. "I really think I'd rather stay," he said.

Jorf's eyes flickered.

"Really," Art protested. "Business is shot anyhow. If I didn't join today it'd be a week or a month from now. What future is there for us?"

Jorf seemed to be calming down. "Maybe you right," he said. "You want go fight THEM?"

This was a question whose answer held many ramifications. For expediency Art said, "Yes."

Jorf embraced him. "You good boy," he said. "You be good. Kill plenty." As abruptly as the Old Man had stormed into the recruiting station he was gone.

The recruiter wiped his forehead. "I wish we could enlist him," he said. "Now . . . you're a diver?"

"I can type sixty words a minute," Art said hopefully.

"I can do ninety," the recruiter said. "What kind of diving have you been doing?"

"Well . . ."

"Hard hat, scuba, snorkel . . . ?"

"Oh uh, well, I'm not certificated but I can work hard hat or scuba."

"And you prefer not to go into detail about what you've been doing and where you've been doing it?"

"Well . . ."

"How deep have you worked?"

"Maybe a hundred meters."

"Do you enjoy it?"

"It was a living."

"We don't get too many men with diving experience," the recruiter said.

Art had a feeling he wasn't going to like what came next.

"It's about the nearest you can come to operating outside a ship in zero gravity."

Art knew he had been right.

"At least there aren't any sharks or rip tides out there."

"I'm a whiz at alphabetical filing too," Art volunteered.

"So are twelve million women."

"I'm pretty good at languages," Art said desperately.

"Oh?" This time the recruiter seemed interested. He switched to English. When Art didn't stumble he tried French. When the recruiter had exhausted his languages he called in one of the blondish guards. Art bungled his way through enough Polish and Russian to satisfy the guard.

"And you speak Arabic too?" the recruiter asked.

"Very badly," Art hastened. "I've only been around Arabs for a few months. It's a very difficult language."

"You were doing quite well a moment ago," the recruiter said.

"Well uh, that's Moroccan dialect, practically unintelligible in other Arab countries."

The recruiter gave him a doubtful look and switched unexpectedly to German. Art began to relax, seeing visions of a cozy future somewhere in a headquarters where he could smooth the paths of power between various high commands.

The recruiter hmmmed and made cryptic marks on Art's application form. "Yes," he said absently. "Six weeks' training in cislunar orbit and then we'll see where personnel puts you."

"In space?" Art was horrified.

"You enlisted to fight, didn't you?"

"Oh yes," Art said hurriedly. "But I thought there'd be something on Earth . . ."

"Let us pray it never comes to that," the recruiter said grimly.

The thing Art remembered mostly about the next six weeks was constant terror. He had supposed the training would be by one of the aliens sent along with the overage ships but so far Art had never seen an offworlder in the flesh. The training station was commanded by a washed-out astronaut, who, in the recruits' opinion, still had both feet planted firmly on the ground.

Nobody else did. The station was a string of plastic-coated fabric bags, which, with a pound and a half of atmosphere, inflated like a string of sausages. During Art's stay enough were added to complete a two-kilometer circle. Once the ends were joined, incoming bags were used to create spokes. This helped ease the constant traffic through compartments where somebody was struggling for a few moments of restless, zero grav sleep. There were times after the spokes were fitted when Art managed to sleep for an hour at a time before thrashing to sweaty wakefulness with his recurrent nightmare of falling.

Mostly though, he read through the sleep periods, devouring bales of science-fiction paperbacks, hunting for a clue to how a red-blooded American draft dodger could have ended up training to fight a war in space. Though he read from Pohl to Poul, he found no clue.

But he got used to zero grav. It was harder to get used to sponging up stray and ropy gobs of the breakfast each new recruit discovered he hadn't really wanted even before he ate it.

Art had thought he would suffer from claustrophobia in these quarters with all their sounds and smells. Then one day he had been issued a life suit. The instant he passed out through the airlock he knew the recruiter had been wrong. Maybe somewhere in the universe life outside could be likened to scuba diving. But not here, not with Earth taking up half the sky—not with Art scrabbling madly to hang onto the airlock's grabstrap. Intellect could deduce that a man in orbit could not fall. But intellect could not tell his paralyzed body that he wasn't a thousand miles above where he ought to be, with not even air between him and something hard that he was going to hit even harder the instant he let go.

The instructor pried his fingers loose one by one. Curled into a fetal ball with arms about his head, Art felt himself being dragged off into space. Within a week he came grudgingly to admit that at least there were no sharks or rip tides. As long as he didn't look down at Earth—as long as he kept his mind on whatever chore he was up to at the moment, it really was like diving in some totally calm, perfectly transparent sea, except that he could not swim. It took a while to get the knack of pointing a thruster backward and coming anywhere near where one wanted to go.

Finally six weeks were up and, though Art never got over being frightened, at least his fear was controllable. He found himself interpreting for the recruits who arrived each day on vomit-slimed shuttles, projecting a calm he had never been able to feel himself. There were times when he thought he would never be free from the importunings of recruits who spoke no recognizable languages:

timid, fresh-caught jungle creatures whose vomit smelled of exotic spices.

He wondered if he would become part of the boot camp's permanent personnel. The ten months had dwindled to seven. Earth equipment had not yet spotted THEM but crews aboard ships already transferred to Earth command had no difficulty spotting a tiny afterimage which instruction manuals said was the track where a large object or group thereof had jumped into hyperspace.

When Art asked how the holo could see images years before light could travel the interstellar distances, he was given an explanation which proved the instructor knew less Einstein than Art did. Not wishing to spend more hours sponging up vomit, Art thanked him and did not ask for elaboration. Next waking period he was called to the personnel office.

Personnel was on the rim of the wheel which by now had been given a slight spin. The artificial gravity was enough to keep him from drifting off the bench where he waited with a half dozen older men who all seemed in the terminal stages of various illnesses. For one mad hopeful moment Art thought he was being sent back home, down to Earth.

Somehow Vietnam and Cambodia and all the other little undeclared wars had been quietly shelved. But despite Watergate, Nixon was still very much alive. Art couldn't go home. Maybe he could wangle his way into the French part of the Pacific where divers could make a living and the computers were still lackadaisical enough for a man to survive without a pedigree.

He wondered what Jorf was doing nowadays. He supposed his conscience ought to bother him for having left just when everything was coming apart. The Old Man had saved his life. But he had put in six arduous dangerous months with the Old Man. They ought to be square. But he couldn't help thinking . . . if it hadn't been for Jorf . . .

The aging derelicts went into the personnel office and came out with longer faces. Finally it was Art's turn. The personnel man was English. He riffled through Art's dossier and hawed. "Ummmnnn-yeeeeesss," he began. "Despite some initial reluctance you've shaped up rather well, Jansen. What would you like to do now?"

Two months had taught Art the wisdom of never answering that kind of question. "Whatever the Alliance thinks best," he said.

"Wellsaid," the personnel man wheezed. "Ah, ummnn-yeeeeessssss. Been hiding your light under a bushel, I see."

"I can type sixty words per minute."

Personnel apparently had not heard him. "Isn't often we get a special request like this. Absolutely insists you're indispensable for smooth operation of the command. Ever hear of the *Nishrub?*"

"The what, sir?"

"*Nishrub*. Fleet waterboat."

"Oh." That, Art guessed, was why, in Arabic, its name meant "we drink."

"Captain says he remembers your splendid work and—"

In Arabic! "I really am a whiz at alphabetical filing," Art said. But he knew it was no use. An hour later he was boarding a shuttle for the holding orbit out where the fleet was parked.

Jorf was wearing a jump suit instead of a *djellaba* when Art boarded the *Nishrub*. "Ahtt!" he roared, and enveloped him in a bear hug. "Just like old days. This time we kill plenty."

"I thought this was a tanker."

Jorf's exultation was momentarily dampened. "Yah," he agreed. "No arms."

"What kind of crew?"

"Shitbirds. People come from nowhere. But one thing I make sure. Everyone is sailor. No goddam sheepherders. You be Talker just like old days."

Art tried to smile. In a way he really was glad to see the Old Man again. Jorf never asked anyone to do anything he wasn't ready to do himself. If only he weren't ready to do so many things . . .

So his escape had come full circle. Art reminded himself that the *Nishrub* was noncombatant. He spent a day exploring. The tanker was shaped like an eight-hundred-meter-long sleeping pill, a round-ended cylinder one hundred ninety meters in diameter. Her length was divided into five tanks with a central companionway for pumping machinery and human passage. Engines and crew quarters took up a tiny, nearly invisible bulge at one end of the capsule. Finally he was satisfied there really were no weapons aboard, unless one counted the diver's knives the crew carried.

They had the weathered look of men who have spent hard lives in the open. He wondered how Jorf had circumvented the Alliance's equal opportunity edict. The *Nishrub*'s crew were of every shape and color. But they were all men.

And now they were all on the losing side, waiting for the hovering THEM ship to strike.

Jorf glanced up from the holo. "What's temperature?" he asked.

"Numbers 1 to 3 are down to 2 degrees. Number 4 is 2.4 degrees. Number 5 is only 10 per cent full and still 5 degrees."

Jorf gave a noncommittal grunt.

Art worried. The tanker's water was already expanding. Once it reached zero and ice crystals began forming the expansion would accelerate. He knew the tanker had been built to take it but he was nervous about putting unnecessary strains on old equipment. "You sure we couldn't use just a little heat?" he asked.

"No power," Jorf said.

Art guessed the Old Man was right. But agonized shrieks of shifting metal were already coming from the forward section. He had a sudden idea. "Look, the fleet doesn't need this water any more. Maybe if we pumped it out while it's still liquid—"

Jorf gazed levelly at him.

"Well, we may be out here a long time and I was thinking, if we emptied tanks and got soil from these rocks maybe we could plant gardens and . . ."

It had seemed a good idea when he started talking. Under the Old Man's level stare it didn't sound good at all. Art wondered why. The Old Man wasn't any technical whiz. Art was willing to bet he hadn't the foggiest idea of how the *Nishrub*'s nuclear drive worked, or how to navigate if the shipboard computers failed. He steeled himself to try again but Jorf was still staring at him. "We keep water," he said.

Art knew when to shut up. His breath was starting to fog. Abruptly he realized no power meant not even the tiny amount needed to heat the living quarters. "Is it okay to keep using the heat in life suits?" he asked.

Jorf thought a moment. "Yah, but no shitbirds breathing in radio." He passed a hand over the stubble on his head and thought a moment. "Call officers," he said.

Art's hand was halfway to the mike when he remembered. He

kicked off down the companionway. There were only four officers aboard. And Jorf was already on the bridge. Art found one mate writing what was obviously a Last Letter Home. The other stank of whisky and *kif* but he came awake easily enough when Art shook him. Farther down the companionway he found the engineering officer's cubicle empty. He thought a moment. With engines and power secured there was no use going aft.

He forced rust-stiffened hinges on the opening between living quarters and the rest of the companionway that went the whole eight hundred meters through the middle of the *Nishrub*'s tanks. The creaks and groans of complaining metal were louder here. He pulled his weightless way past now quiet pumping machinery, past access plates and inspection holes. The engineering officer was up in the bow checking strain gauges. "*Buon giorno, Arturo,*" he said.

"Hi. *Il vecchio ti chiama.*"

"Ah?" The engineering officer took a final look and began pulling his way aft.

"*Problèmi?*" Art asked.

"Not yet. Of course, it's only started expanding." A bulkhead shrieked like Hitler in Brooklyn. Art tried not to look worried.

The engineering officer was a cheerful, bull-necked man from a part of the world which changes nationality once each generation. He spoke North Italian, South Slav, and far-out German; and was known sometimes as Bercovici, others as Berkóvich, and occasionally as Bergson. When a recruiter had inquired his religious preference Heinrich Bercovici had replied, "Botulist." He preceded Art through the stiff-hinged door and back to the bridge.

The two mates were already there. Art wondered if he should have called the storekeeper. The storekeeper was not an officer but he might be needed in a council of war. Art was heading back out when Jorf said, "Stay."

He drifted to a corner and tried to make himself inconspicuous. He knew the mates were suspicious of his long acquaintance with the Old Man. He wondered what they would say if he ever told them how eagerly he wished he were somewhere—anywhere else. The short one had once been nakhoda on a dhow sailing from Aden down the Zanzibar coast. He was a shiny black man with a sharp Nilotic face twisted into a constant scowl. Coming from the opposite end of the

Arab world, he had great trouble getting Jorf to understand his Arabic. Since he was perennially suspicious of Art's interpreting, he spoke a hodgepodge of English interlarded with Koranic quotations. He was haranguing the other mate at the moment, dwelling on his years of piloting dhows.

"Right, Nessim," the other mate grinned. "I'll consult you the next time we have to take in sail." The other mate was a cheerful man from Belfast whose relations with Nessim were complicated by some ancient history about a wife or daughter.

Jorf grunted and Art caught that flicker of his eye . . . like a gamecock's. Could the Old Man really have a nictitating membrane? Both mates were abruptly silent.

"So . . ." the Old Man began. "Now what we do?"

The silence was uninterrupted. Art wondered if he ought to bring up his idea about emptying the tanks and raising food again.

"What's the news from Earth?" McQuoyd finally asked.

Jorf glanced at Art.

"Without power I can't crank up the receiver," Art said. "If we were on the sunward side of this rock maybe . . ."

"*Ch'hal—*" Nessim began, then with a glare at Art he switched to English. "How many ship Allies got?"

Jorf squinted again at the holo. "One," he said.

"Big one, many guns?"

"Little one, no guns."

"He means this one, you Wog curracher."

Nessim drew himself to an erect dignity at some forty-five degrees to the Belfast mate. "I am not westernized oriental gentleman," he sneered. "But my people write The Book before your muddy island—"

Jorf grunted again.

"Where's the nearest THEM?" McQuoyd asked.

"Maybe thousand kilometers."

"Coming back toward us?"

"Still moving on."

With the Allied fleet destroyed, Art realized THEM no longer had any reason to reverse direction. If they continued on toward Earth, maybe after they were out of the immediate neighborhood the *Nishrub* could sneak away.

"Where we go?" Nessim asked.

"Where we want go?" Jorf corrected.

Silence again. The Alliance home planets had been attacked once because a captured ship had carried a full set of charts. There were no charts aboard the *Nishrub* that would give the slightest hint which way to head in search of a civilized planet. There was no woman aboard the *Nishrub*. Now Art knew why the Old Man had given him that level stare when he had suggested gardening. He remembered all the lovely Swedish girls down in Marbella to get warm. Knowing he would never warm another, Art wondered if the other men were as near tears as he was.

Jorf's gaze flickered to Bercovici. "That big sonofabitch—how fast he turn?"

The engineering officer shrugged. "Who knows what THEM ships can do? If they really can't go into hyperspace this close to a sun, I guess they're bound by the same physics as we are."

"Can he turn faster?"

"Than us? Who knows? Depends on what size engines."

Art felt a thrill of horror as he realized what this conversation was leading to. "No!" It slipped out of him without his meaning it to.

Jorf looked at him.

"What chance do you think we have? This is only a waterboat. We have no rockets. Look what happened to every Alliance fighting ship that went up against THEM . . ." He trailed off, feeling himself wither under the stares of the other three.

"Perhaps you'd like to go back to Earth?" The Belfast mate had a bogtrotter brogue he could lay on at will.

"Do you really think we can do it?" Nessim asked. He was ignoring Art and speaking Arabic now.

Jorf shrugged and his eyes flickered. "So what if we don't?"

"How?" McQuoyd asked. But the Old Man was looking at the engineering officer.

Bercovici studied dials and punched a computer. When the power-less computer failed to react he swore a complicated trilingual oath and found a slide rule. "No power?" he asked.

"Not yet," Jorf said. "Still too close."

"Hokay," Bercovici said. "Maybe five hours."

"Good. Enough time tell everybody. Ahtt!"

"Yessir?"

"Everybody check suit, get full air bottles."

"You're going to pump the water out?" Art asked.

"Pump hell!" Jorf growled. "Go tell men."

"But what should I tell them?"

"We gonna fight."

Art took a deep breath and pushed out of the bridge. He knew that in a moment he was going to faint. But, unlucky as usual, he didn't. He wondered what swift communion had intuited between the Old Man and Bercovici. All he could think of was the way those green lights in the holo had flared and gone out. It was such a futile gesture. Maybe by some miracle they could damage one ship. What difference would it make? A hundred ninety-nine others would still flatten every man-made structure on Earth.

Maybe it was different for the older men. They had lived their lives. Maybe, Art thought, years from now he would have wished he'd ended it all with one magnificent gesture instead of spending the rest of his days cockroaching about the galaxy watching his comrades die off one by one, or kill each other for the remaining food. But not now. He was only twenty-three years old. Even without that Alliance snake-oil salesman he would've had a good fifty years left to warm the Swedish winter out of those lovely lissome blondes who invaded Spain each year. Now he was going to die in some harebrained suicide mission. It just wasn't fair.

CHAPTER FOUR

Scribbled on the pyramids are the still legible graffiti of Alexander's nice Greek boys who were unimpressed with a country where even the buildings leaned. Twenty-five hundred years later Art could still not answer their question: "What am I doing here?"

Even before the Alliance, life on Earth had been growing increasingly weird. Art's grandfather had fled a dim future as a Scandinavian farmhand, lured to the New World with promises of free land. Art's father had been forced off that land at a time when everyone else seemed to be prospering—except small farmers who couldn't raise the hundred thousand to mechanize a farm into a food factory. Art's father drifted into town and became a bartender.

And Art . . . It wasn't exactly a generation gap but things were different now in a subtly mystifying way. As the old man put it after an evening of fumbling, "When I was a kid we laughed but somewhere inside we still *believed.*" The business of war involved believing. Earlier breeds of snake-oil salesmen had convinced Americans they were a peace-loving nation, despite available statistics re the years of peace *vs.* war since 1776.

One pince-nezzed con man convinced us that the US of A's divinely inspired foreign policy was for the good of all mankind and that only hopelessly perverted and evil minds steeped in the insidiously poisoned juices of Fu Manchu could take advantage of a fleet so invitingly laid out one Sunday morning for them to sink. We *believed.*

Even Art's old man found it hard to believe in divine inspiration for Vietnam and Cambodia. Art went to college because it beat the Army. Choosing a curriculum was something else. As a child he had learned bits of Swedish from his grandparents. And the old French lady next door had taught him whatever it is they speak in

Quebec. The college was offering Russian. Art guessed it would be the easiest way out.

Then he learned college students were forced to take all sorts of unbelievably tedious subjects. Even this would have been acceptable if there had not been a totally unreasonable expectation that one would actually study this drivel. Art survived one semester, then applied for a grant to the culturally deprived, creating a story whose only basis in fact was that his grandparents had spoken rather poor English.

With the proceeds he had taken a charter flight and traded the return half of his ticket to a devotee of free enterprise who hung around the American Express in Antwerp. Two months later, because a lissome Swedish lass of whom he was tiring and an inept young German with but one thing on their minds had run into linguistic difficulties trying to translate "My place or yours?", he ended up scuba diving on the Costa del Sol.

The German's place turned out to be docked at Estepona. When Art's linguistic talent had smoothed the way for the two lovers he found himself invited along. Once aboard, it took him all of ten minutes to realize the yacht was not cruising for pleasure.

Art guessed they were going to smuggle cigarettes or perhaps something more profitable. He found the handbooks and started learning how to use scuba gear. Later that night as the diesel racketed into a choppy Mediterranean he reflected that, for smuggling, the crew had been recruited without much screening. They were all young, from half a dozen northern countries, and a week ago they had all been strangers. Art guessed he was imagining the smuggling operation.

A day later near a tiny rock with an Arab name and a Spanish flag he learned they were diving for Roman remains.

"*Nicht ungesetzlich,*" the German had explained; not illegal, but governments had an annoying habit of jumping in with both feet whenever some amateur archaeologist found a promising site and . . . well, wouldn't it really be best just to keep it to ourselves and be spared all the inconveniences of reporters and claim jumpers?

When Art learned the going price for a genuine Roman captain's chair he decided they might as well salvage the wreck before reporting it. By then he had been aboard twenty-four hours, had read everything available about scuba gear, had tried on a suit, and considered himself as expert as anyone else aboard. It turned out he was something more of an expert. Since nobody else had read the instructions Art made the first dive.

Later when he had gathered more experience in murky waters Art wondered what combination of advance knowledge and blind luck had brought him directly over a two-thousand-year-old wreck on his first dive. He was poking around the dim depths trying to figure how to raise a crud-encrusted bronze anchor when a sudden grinding noise startled him.

Peering upward, he saw the wavery outline of the yacht's hull. It was a moment before he realized the noise was from a turning propellor. He wondered what was wrong. Perhaps he ought to start back up to the surface. It was at least ninety feet and he guessed he'd have to decompress somewhere along the way. Before he could make up his mind the yacht's wavery outline moved majestically northwest, bearing away his pocketknife, his clothes, his wallet, and—his passport.

Halfway to the surface he was hanging onto the buoy rope taking deep breaths and forcing himself not to hurry through decompression when another larger hull passed overhead, making an even greater grinding noise. This hull had three propellors. The buoy rocked madly and the rope came out of his hands. He guessed he had decompressed long enough. By the time he reached the surface the German's yacht was long gone. The larger boat was disappearing in the haze to northwest, leaving behind a stench of diesel that smelled oddly of garlic.

Art did not ponder over his past sins. He was too busy correlating the distance to the nearest land with the amount of air left in his tanks. He supposed when he ran out he could cut them loose and swim on the surface. The wet suit was supposed to lend some buoyancy and with flippers . . . But forty miles was a damn long walk without food or rest. He suspected it might be even longer to swim. Meanwhile he might as well stay out of the chop and take advantage of what air he had. He consulted a wrist compass and began swimming, surfacing occasionally to look for land that he knew was not there.

His hour was nearly up when he heard the drone of a motor. The German had managed to lose the patrol and was circling to pick him up. The motor slowed and stopped. Moments later an anchor chain rattled. Art began swimming toward the sound.

A hundred meters away he saw it was not the German yacht that had taken him to this busy piece of water. Strange ragged men lounged on deck. Art heard a raucous laugh and a phrase that sounded just like those Moorish wailings that leaked into Spain from Arab radio just across the straits. He wished he knew how to speak Arabic—at least how to yell for help. He was taking his mouthpiece out when something snapped in the water beside his head and an instant later he heard the crack of a rifle.

Art was unused to violence. When a bullet narrowly missed his head his reaction was normal: he simply didn't believe it was for real. "Knock it off, you crazy sonofabitch!" he yelled, "I'm an American." In extenuation it can only be said that he had been out of the States so short a time that he had not yet learned to hide behind that large red maple leaf that adorns the knapsacks of so many English speakers in Europe. But his shout got immediate results. A large man wearing a turban and three days' growth of grizzled beard knocked the rifle from the other's hands and yelled, *"Qu'est ce que vous faites avec ma naufrage?"* His accent was worse than Art's.

Art was being pulled over the rail before it occurred to him that if this wreck belonged to the Arabs and he had been poaching—oh well . . . too late now. The large grizzled man was still cuffing the other who had held the rifle. Now he turned and repeated his question. "What the hell you do my wreck?"

And that was how Art met Jorf.

Since then hardly a day had gone by that Art had not wished he had never heard of the impetuous Moor. Right now aboard the *Nishrub* certain possibilities were beginning to soak into his unwilling mind. Jorf had been asking the engineering officer how fast THEM could turn. And for several hours now the heat had been turned off. The *Nishrub*'s water was freezing. Bulkheads were shrieking. No, Art didn't want to think about it at all. He forced his mind back to that other stress-filled day in the middle of the Med when he had first met Jorf.

Art had been in the water too long and the chill had gotten to him. At least he liked to think it was the chill, for while Jorf and the others wrangled over whether to kill him before or after questioning, Art quietly fainted.

It has been observed that the olfactory sense is most closely connected with the emotions, that a sudden smell can arouse long dead memories and passions. When Art came to, the heat and racketing engines convinced him that he was still alive. Indefinable stenches of bilge, unfamiliar cooking, ancient fish, and unbathed humanity made him wonder momentarily if life were all that good. Then his innate respect for his own survival came to the fore again. He struggled not to vomit. From somewhere there came a thread of cool fresh air. He twisted his head to catch it.

Like many boats built in warm climes, the *Fatma* had been designed without thought for crew. There was space for engines, for fuel, for cargo. The crew slept in odd corners atop mats or piles of rags. Someone had put Art in a warm space next to one of the two small engines that lay like nursing cubs beside a much larger engine. He lay in a pleasant daze trying not to think unpleasant thoughts. After an hour Jorf stuck his head through a hole in the bulkhead. "I don't know anything," Art said.

"Like hell you don't!" Jorf said. "You know you alive; them others dead."

"Dead?" Art echoed. He didn't know whether the demise of these faithless friends troubled him as much as the loss of his passport.

"Unless they swim damn good." Jorf shrugged. "Your boat on Alborán rocks. Maybe Spanish lighthouse man get them."

Art guessed he ought to be grateful. At least he was alive.

"You good diver?"

Art suspected it would not be in his best interest to admit he had made only one dive. "I'm out of air," he said.

"We got compressor. You want work?"

Art nodded, then caution overtook him. "Is it legal?" he asked. "How much money?"

"Plenty money."

Art decided that was enough answer for now. From somewhere on deck came sounds of cooking. He followed Jorf through the hole in the bulkhead and saw a man cooking stew over a brazier alee of the pilot house. Moments later Art was digging in with his right hand like everybody else. Halfway through the meal he realized the cook was the man who had shot at him. The cook grinned and pointed at the stew. *"Tadjim,"* he said.

Within a week Art knew two hundred words of what he thought was Arabic until he went ashore at Tetuán and saw an Egyptian movie. Then he learned the Moroccan audience understood eastern Arabic no better than a Spaniard follows Italian. He wondered if it would actually be possible to read these bewildering pothooks. Familiar emblems like Shell, Mobil, Coca-Cola—all were recognizable by shape and color. But instead of the familiar words each had meaningless squiggles. Then one day he saw that both the Shell and Mobil logos began in the same shaped symbol.

Illogical, until he remembered many languages read from right to left. The same backward L-J squiggle also occurred on the bottle of warm Coke he was drinking. He found paper and a pencil. One day Jorf saw him trying to separate the words on the side of a plastic British Petroleum bottle. The grizzled man began teaching Art to read.

Art had assumed he would go to work salvaging the Roman wreck but he didn't. Instead they drifted days on end in the fog, occasionally going through the motions of fishing, though any luck would have been embarrassing since the fish hold was nearly filled with a third engine much larger than the other two which normally drove the decrepit boat. One day a freighter passed quite close. Next day Jorf began a square search which ended when he sighted a small plastic jug.

Jorf put away his binoculars and turned to Art. "You dive now," he said.

"What do I look for?"

"Follow rope down. Tie heavy line to what you find on bottom. We pull up."

Feeling queasy, Art got into his wet suit. He guessed he had no reason to complain. He had volunteered for something like this when he went aboard the German's yacht. Now he was doing it for another employer. Without a passport there was no place to go. He'd better stay on the good side of these Arabs.

When he got to the bottom there were several plastic-covered packages with rope loops ready for convenient lifting. Art had always assumed the stuff he was diving for would come in small and easily concealed packages. These were surprisingly large and heavy. He tied a rope to one and jerked. The package rose from the mud bottom, stirring up a cloud which brought several inquisitive fish. The rope came back down and he connected it to the next package. Finally he tied the rope to the last of the five packages and began working his way back up. When they helped him over the rail one package was already open. He didn't know whether to be frightened or relieved. The package contained small arms ammunition.

Even then Art hadn't been too perturbed until he saw the crew produce automatic weapons from some hidden armory. Each man fired several rounds and ran through interminable drills to make sure their weapons wouldn't jam. Jorf saw Art's nervousness and smiled. He disappeared into the pilot house and a moment later reappeared with a weapon which he tossed.

Art had never seen one before but he'd seen pictures. And even without the pictures he could transliterate the Russian letters which meant ARP-47. He wondered if he shouldn't have tried to swim home that day the Germans abandoned him.

"Good gun," Jorf said. "You gonna like."

"What makes you think I want to join the Commies?"

Jorf laughed. "You gotta learn," he said. "If guns American, *then* you know Russians behind it."

Art reflected on some of the dirty linen recently laundered by Senate committees. "So these arms come courtesy of somebody else?"

Jorf nodded.

"For this I ducked Vietnam," Art muttered. "Who are we fighting?"

"You see."

That was what Art was afraid of. Why did he always have to end up in the middle of something like this? Nobody ever seemed to want a fight. Yet the wars went on. Art suspected this was not one of those things he was going to understand when he was older.

Right now aboard the *Nishrub* he was almost a year older and he still couldn't see why all these men who had a good chance of living—if they'd just be quiet and not make waves—why were they all so hot to trot on a suicide mission? Nobody could possibly believe it would make any difference. So they got one THEM ship— Big deal! He wondered if they were romantics who dreamed of immortality in song and legend. Screw it. Art would be content with postponing his mortality another fifty years.

Back aboard Jorf's *Fatma* it had looked as if he might not live fifty minutes. Even now he could not look back and find any logic in the unpredictable Moor's actions. Life had settled into an un-settling routine of loading in North African ports, crossing the hundred-odd miles to Spain and lying offshore. Usually Art didn't know what was in the waterproofed packages they were transporting. The rest of the time he preferred not to know.

Jorf's relations with Spanish fishermen who accepted the mer-chandise were friendly and informal. His relations with anyone re-motely connected with government were something else.

Art had camped along the Spanish coast. He had learned that any-one camping on the beach would be visited by the funny-hatted *guardias civiles,* always polite, always proper. He had found it reas-suring to live in a country where crime was so nonexistent that a stolen car made headlines. Now he understood what the *guardia civil* was doing all night on those beaches.

The Spanish *guardacostas* was equally active, making any rendez-vous with fishing boats risky. Often the crew of Jorf's *Fatma* would work frantically tossing merchandise over the side, fixing plastic jug buoys which rode several meters below the surface, invisible to the coast guard and anyone else, save a fishing boat out dragging a beam trawl. Moments later when a patrol boat appeared Jorf and his men would be peacefully tending their own nets.

Art had learned enough Arabic by now to hold his own with the ob-scene and ungrammatical crew. He could read and pronounce the names that were painted on the *Fatma* at least once a week. Like the others, he learned to ignore them. Nobody seemed deliberately to be holding back but he still didn't know what was going on. Questions elicited blank stares or laughter. Occasionally he had to dive for ship-ments on the bottom off the African coast. He wondered why this kind of thing couldn't be dropped off Spain instead of being trans-shipped in Jorf's boat but guessed it had something to do with the curiosity that would be aroused if freighters deviated from shipping lanes.

He knew it was dangerous and illegal. If only he had a passport . . . but that entailed going to an American consulate. There would be questions about draft status and . . . Jorf had fixed him up with seaman's papers which allowed him brief trips ashore in Spain and Morocco but seamen were viewed with increasing suspicion as they strayed from the dock area. Like it or not, Art was tied to the Arabs.

One day a patrol boat appeared. Art was puzzled. They had unloaded hours ago but tension grew aboard the *Fatma*. The weather was hazy and Spanish radar not all that good. Even if they had been carrying controversial cargo Jorf could always cut in the third, undeclared engine and outrun the patrol. But he wasn't doing it.

Art had learned to dread that bird-of-prey stare from eyes that flickered almost as if Jorf had a nictitating membrane. He was more worried when he saw the grizzled skipper climb into a wet suit for the first time. "Hurry up," Jorf said.

Art began getting into his own scuba gear. "What's going on?" he asked.

Jorf glanced briefly at the cook, who usually did the diving. "Butterfingers," he growled, leaving Art to wonder how that word had crept into his limited English.

The others were getting the net over the side to go through the motions of fishing. As the patrol boat loomed out of the mist aport Jorf and Art slipped over the starboard side. They swam under the *Fatma* and Jorf began hacking at a slight bulge to one side of the keel. Still wondering, Art drew his own knife and began cutting away the plastic foam. Inside was a dinner plate-sized something or other. Jorf struggled but most of the flotation had been chopped away and the thing was dragging him down. Art sheathed his knife and between them they managed to transfer it to the patrol boat. Jorf peeled off plastic to expose a clean sticky surface. While Art was wondering what would stick this neatly underwater the skipper made certain adjustments and beckoned. They swam rapidly back under their own boat.

Art had assumed they would stay underwater until the Spanish patrol boat went away but Jorf was making unmistakable gestures. They surfaced at the edge of the net and were helped aboard under the suspicious eyes of the *guardacostas* crew. Jorf put on his used car salesman's smile and escorted the boarding party around.

In retrospect Art could never imagine how such a small mine could do so much damage. The center of the patrol boat went skyward in a sheet of flame and Art felt the heat before the concussion knocked him down. The *guardacostas* broke into pieces and burning oil crept toward the *Fatma*. The Spanish boarding party stared aghast. Jorf produced his diving knife and almost leisurely drew it across the throat of the *teniente de corveta*. It seemed to Art that the others were needlessly prodigal of ammunition as they emptied magazines into twitching bodies.

He stared, not believing. This was movie stuff. Things like this didn't really happen. In a moment he would awaken and it would all be just another of those nightmares he'd been having ever since he came to associate with these unpredictable Arabs. Even while he was helping tie weights to the bloody corpses he still didn't believe it had really happened.

They scoured the sea for fragments of the patrol boat. Since it had been steel-hulled there weren't too many. Several crewmen had for unknown reasons been wearing life jackets. They weighted the bodies and sent them to join the boarding party. When they were satisfied no wreckage could identify the patrol boat Jorf got under way.

Art was coming out of his daze, feeling sicker by the minute. "Why?" he asked the beaming cook. "Those poor bastards were just doing their job."

Jorf heard him. "They do something my father when I am little boy in Rif," he said.

Art decided if he ever got close to a bookstore he'd read up on the history of Spanish colonialism. That night they docked at a Spanish port but a planeload of Swedish girls had just arrived to bake the Scandinavian winter from their long and well-shaped bones and Art was too busy to remember bookstores.

Next day as they were heading back toward the African side Jorf was relaxed and expansive. Art too was satiated after his night ashore. "I don't get it," he said in his now passable Arabic. "You're friendly with Spaniards, you speak Spanish, you made a Spanish port."

Jorf gave a canariphagous smile. "We waited for that particular boat a long time," he said, and Art knew the subject was closed. He would have been more inclined to forget it if he and Jorf had not spent a day installing another limpet mine in the vacant spot next to the *Fatma*'s keel.

He slipped into a timeless dream world, not knowing whether his free-floating anxiety was greater afloat or ashore. His American clothes had gone the way of his passport. People who bothered to be curious about such things assumed he was another of those blond French *colons* who had rejected de Gaulle and gone Arab with a vengeance.

His parents still assumed he was doing the student bit in Europe, and would be home for the next term. He wrote interesting bits of fiction about cathedrals and museums and wondered how to break the news that he could never come back until Nixon was impeached, assassinated, exiled to Paris, or wherever politicians went in their next incarnation.

"Don't worry," Jorf consoled. "Soon plenty money. You buy nice black girl."

"I've always been partial to blondes," Art said.

"Hokay, so you buy blonde."

"Where do they sell them?"

Jorf gave him an odd look.

Ashore somebody had sighted that damned thing that was going to hit Earth in a few months unless . . . and then the organic matter had hit the fan with the alien ambassador's arrival. Jorf's business had gone to hell and the first thing Art knew he had escaped into the Alliance armed forces, away from this trigger-happy Arab who shot up patrol boats for the fun of it instead of running and hiding like any self-respecting smuggler with an eye for a deutschmark.

And now he was back with a shipful of weirdos bound together only by their universal disregard for their own lives. Art wondered if he was the only man aboard the *Nishrub* with an intelligent concern for his own skin.

A bulkhead groaned and shrieked as the ice behind it expanded. The bridge was getting cold. Art's breath exhaled in cottony puffs as he tried to stay out of the way. He turned up his suit rheostat but still he could not stop shivering.

There was an odd two-toned thumping coming over his suit radio. He ignored the wrangling in the bridge and turned up the sound. The THEM ship was so close he was picking up internal communications. He wondered if these drumming sounds were language or a garbled TV signal. Either way the *Nishrub* was far too close for any noncombatant—especially for any Art happened to be aboard. He wondered if the others were hearing it.

Bercovici didn't seem worried. *"È possibile,"* he said cheerfully. "If it takes THEM as long to set up for a jump as it does us . . ." With his mind in neutral Art interpreted.

The mates were muttering at each other. "She was gentle and fair," McQuoyd said reminiscently. "Now how was I to know she could possibly be related to an ugly old man like—"

Art interposed himself before Nessim could make up in mayhem what he lacked in blarney. He wondered why Nessim picked these eternal arguments when invariably the dark man came out the loser. But now they were all losers.

Think positive thoughts, Art told himself. But he couldn't remember any. It was like that day ashore in Marbella after they had shot up the patrol boat.

Art had been sitting in a tiny bar amid the *flasköl* signs. He had learned playing something Swedish on the jukebox was the quickest way to let the lissome strangers from the north in on the secret that they shared a language, that he was available and even congenial. A long-haired blonde with legs to match sat at the other end of the bar. She had arrived that same day, Art decided, for she still wore Stockholm instead of the more flamboyant Mediterranean styles. They had not even looked directly at one another yet but Art knew he was communicating. Arab getup was an infallible icebreaker for girls whose only idea of Arab life came from *Peer Gynt*. He had been ready to stroll down to her end of the bar when a *guardia civil* stuck his head in the door.

There was nothing odd about a cop taking a quick look into a bar. In his pocket Art had the seaman's papers Jorf had fixed him up with. The *guardia* pulled his head back out and continued his round but his look aroused a vague uneasiness.

The blonde was looking at Art with open expectation now but that damned *guardia civil* had put his timing off. He wondered if he was imagining things. There was no way they could know. It had to be a guilty conscience. He sipped his beer and tried to get back into it with the blonde.

A pair of noisy English boys entered. She discouraged them, still hoping for action from this exotic young man in Arab dress. Art sipped beer. What name had been painted on the *Fatma*'s bows that day? Whatever, it was long gone. Even if the patrol boat had radioed some message . . .

Art shrugged it off and was ready to concentrate on the blonde when the *guardia civil* returned, this time with another. They gestured peremptorily. Art had seen the *guardia* in action before. He might as well go without multiple contusions.

They took him to the *comandancia,* into a slightly tacky room with wooden benches, where he was left alone. Art sat for an hour. He sat two more hours. Finally a *guardia* opened the inner door and beckoned.

The *comandante* was a dapper man whose hair seemed varnished. He finished fiddling with papers on his desk, then regarded Art mournfully. A minute passed in silence. Art resolved not to be the first to speak. He wondered how much they knew.

"Where do you get the narcotics?" the *comandante* finally asked.

Art stared. The *comandante* made a gesture of annoyance. "*¿Habla español?*"

"If you speak slowly," Art conceded.

"Did you understand the question?"

"No."

The *comandante* repeated slowly, "*¿Dónde consiguen los narcóticos?*"

Art shrugged. "I understand the words."

They fenced for several minutes, the *comandante* picking away while Art told the absolute truth—yes, he had smoked hash a couple of times in Africa, no, never in Spain, because he didn't much care for it, because it was against the law and liquor was cheaper. And no, he had never seen any narcotics aboard Jorf's boat—which was the absolute truth. He had seen all sorts of small and carefully wrapped packages but Art had been careful never to ask what was in them.

Suddenly Art knew what was going to happen. This was the technique Mom had used until Art had learned to anticipate the unexpected question. Seeing the *comandante's* eyes narrow, Art gently deepened his own breathing. Any moment now they would slip him a loaded one about a missing patrol boat.

"Then you have never seen any narcotics aboard the boat which employs you?" the *comandante* persisted.

"Never."

The *comandante's* eyes narrowed. "When," he asked, "was the last time you wrote to your mother?"

Art stared a moment, then burst into relieved laughter. Was that what it was all about? "I don't know. Couple of weeks ago, I guess."

"You were ashore then, with access to a mailbox?"

Art shrugged. "Must have been."

"Then you could not possibly know anything about the wreckage of a missing *guardacostas?*"

Even though he had been prepared Art could not control his face, his respiration. Abruptly there were noises and shouts outside. Thank God, he thought. It sounded like they had come to spring him.

The door opened and he recognized the cook who had once shot at him. Jorf was not there. The cook and two others wore handcuffs.

Art was tossed into a cell with the others. "What in the name of the Merciful and Compassionate is going on?" he asked.

The cook was a small, very dark man with a Senegalese slave somewhere in his family tree. He began spouting nonsense in a singsong voice. After a moment Art realized he was making like a storyteller who squatted in the marketplace and took up a collection from his illiterate audience. The cook was warning Art that the Spanish cops could understand Moroccan dialect and to keep his cotton-picking mouth shut.

The cell's Judas hole opened and closed. A moment later the door opened and Art guessed the interrogation would begin again. Instead, they were escorted to the entrance of the *cuartel*. On the sidewalk Jorf and a thin man in a London-tailored suit were chatting in quiet Arabic. They shook hands with the peculiar Moroccan "give me some skin" gesture and Jorf led his people back to the boat. Behind his smile Art could see the tall man's cold unforgiving anger. Art felt sorry for the *comandante*.

CHAPTER FIVE

It was that same look that worried Art now. Remembering how Jorf had settled his Spanish accounts, Art wondered if determination could avail against automation. "Everybody gets suits ready," the Arab said.

Art's hand went to the intercom before he remembered; no power. He suppressed a shiver and went into the lounge-chow hall. "Check life support gear," he said in half a dozen languages. "Recharge air tanks. And no, I don't know what we're going to do, but the Old Man wants everybody ready." He wished he could disappear for a few minutes but the inexorable bell curves of IQ distribution applied in the asteroid belt just as they did on Earth.

Of the two hundred men aboard, a half dozen had anticipated this command and were ready with immaculate gear and full tanks. The rest were scrambling to comply. And a handful of eight balls stood waiting for him to spell it out. Among them Art saw the moonfaced meat head who polluted radio silence with obscene lyrics in Urdu. He sighed and detailed the high IQ flange of the bell curve to take care of their counterparts.

"No," Jorf said. Startled, Art turned and saw the council of war had ended. Jorf watched the scurrying crewmen. "Smart guys got no time for stupid bastards," Jorf said in English. "Take stupids to help more stupid. They do slow and men learn."

A trifle late for learning, Art suspected, but he realized Jorf's backdoor psychology might be centuries ahead of the sterile crap he had endured in school.

"What do we have in the way of weapons?" Jorf was speaking Arabic again.

He was talking to himself. The skipper always knew these things. "Nothing," Art said. "Unless you count knives."

Jorf frowned. "You forget picks."

It took a moment to realize he meant the alpenstock each man carried to hook himself around outside in zero grav. It had never occurred to Art that these utilitarian instruments could be weapons. He saw Moonface still oblivious of any emergency and floated toward him. "Your air tanks full?"

Moonface smiled and nodded. Art found one bottle empty and the other almost. He herded the singer of obscene songs to the compressor. He studied his own alpenstock. It would puncture suits or skulls. Did THEM wear either? Art's fondest hope had always been that he would never get near enough to find out. He kicked off to the machine shop and joined the line waiting to get at a grinder. A machinist's mate scowled at their bungling efforts and took over.

The blue-eyed man who spoke bad French and worse Arabic cornered Art again. *"Qu'est ce que t'a dit le capitain?"*

"About what?"

"You know. He *tells* you things. What are we going to do?"

"Search me. Looks like we're going to fight."

"Aaaaaaaaaahhhhhh!"

Art was startled. This man actually seemed relieved. Art studied the others sharpening weapons and cheerfully bustling toward oblivion. Was he the only coward left in the Alliance fleet?

"Ahtt!"

He kicked off from a bulkhead and floated back to the bridge. Jorf was huddled again with the mates and the engineering officer. "What's water temperature?"

Art glanced at dials, then remembered the power was off. He kicked off again and grabbed the rusty door that led to the bow eight hundred meters away. Someone had oiled the hinges. Art was pulling his way through when he realized what that meant. He went back and put on his suit.

The water in No. 1 was three tenths of a degree colder. Frost crystals were forming where sensors and other plumbing led in and out. Soon the ice would attain maximum expansion. Art was praying nothing else would happen when he heard another low-pitched groan. He checked his air tanks again before heading back to No. 2.

When he reported Jorf seemed satisfied. The machine shop was busy. Portable rescue saws had been refitted with abrasive disks and men were grinding points and edges on the most improbable tools. One had taken a curve-bladed hand saw from some emergency kit and sharpened the outer curve of the blade. He was happily honing this yataghan while others raided stores for the fist-sized nuts used to close hatches. One man had rigged a slingshot from bungee cord. Others fastened the half-kilo weights to lengths of rope.

They had no gasoline but the pharmacist had broken out medical stores. He was making Molotov cocktails from plasma bottles and alcohol.

"What'd you do with the plasma?" Art asked.

The pharmacist nodded toward the vacuum sink.

Art was aghast. "What if somebody needs a transfusion?"

The pill roller shrugged. "There isn't a hospital or a doctor within a billion miles. What's the point of a transfusion?"

"But can't you—?"

The pill roller was a short Spaniard from up north on the edge of the Basque provinces. He raised his hands expressively. "I can administer purgatives or remove splinters. Anything else's in the hands of that merciful God who looked after His children so carefully during our revolution." He made an expectorating gesture without actually spitting and added, "In the milk of whose Mother I defecate."

Art tried not to think about it. One amateur armorer had altered a battery-powered saw to spin a dozen blades at once. Another was whittling a piece of wood from one of the butterfly net gadgets which were the zero grav equivalent of brooms. Art guessed the Indian was making an *atlatl*. Others were practicing with slings instead of the rigid throwing stick. A shipfitter was brushing up on an old trick for discouraging foremen. He swung a hammer, purposely missing a stanchion. The head broke away and flew bulletlike to dent the far bulkhead. He growled in disgust. He had corrected for a gravity that was not there.

The blue-eyed man caught Art again. "We hit them," he said eagerly. "Do lots of damage, get out quick. Like you say, 'hit and run,' no?"

"Your guess is as good as mine." If the other was right, the pharmacist might soon wish he had his plasma back.

There was a shrieking groan from the tanks up forward, then a high-pitched snap. At first Art thought it was the noise hurting his ears, then there was a clang and the pain eased. He checked to see if his nose was bleeding. When it wasn't, he felt weak-kneed relief. He checked his air for the hundredth time. If they kept letting the water freeze, soon every tank in the hold would rupture. Art hoped there would be enough rusty iron left to hold the *Nishrub* together. Would they be able to keep air in the living space?

Bercovici was struggling to fasten a portable airlock over the hatch. Art helped him with the umbrellalike framework. Finally they had the plastic stuck all around. Bercovici climbed in. Art was following when he heard—

"Ahtt!"

He sighed and helped zip Bercovici in. The pump whirred as he pushed back to the bridge.

"What happen?" Jorf asked. "Berkóvich leave like cork from champagne."

"We've ruptured a tank." Art was never sure how much this Moorish enigma understood of practical engineering. "You've lost hull integrity," he persisted. "Air went zapping out through the crack and the rush pulled the hatch shut. Last time I saw Bercovici he was pumping to reduce pressure so he could open it again and go see how bad things are. So long as you keep letting the water freeze they're bound to get worse."

Jorf remained impassive. "No. 1 froze solid?" he asked.

Art was saved by Bercovici's entry. "Hokay," he said cheerfully. "No. 2 any minute."

Art wondered why an engineering officer could be happy watching his ship come to pieces.

Jorf caught a stanchion and spun to face Art. "Can we make bombs?"

"Out of what?"

"You college boy. You know what makes bang."

Art wondered if Jorf had ever heard of *The Little Red Schoolbook*. He drifted out of the bridge before the skipper could dream up some other request.

The line in the machine shop had shortened. Men were putting finishing touches to makeshift knives. A machinist's mate had torn apart some welding equipment and was fiddling with pipes and hoses. Another was unhooking the safety webbing from a cache of oxygen and acetylene bottles. "Can you make any kind of bombs?" Art asked.

"Does it look like I'm recharging my lighter?" the machinist snapped. Before Art could answer they drifted and bumped into the after bulkhead. It was only a tenth of a G but Art had been weightless so long that the acceleration seemed shockingly heavy. Considering the *Nishrub*'s power-weight ratio, it was. He hoped Jorf had changed his mind and was putting distance between them and THEM. There was another groan as the ship reacted to multiple strains of acceleration and expanding water. Art float-walked up to see what new deviltry the pharmacist was up to.

The bulkheads of sick bay were sooty. Paint blistered like Art's back the first time he stayed too long in the Mediterranean sun. A smell of ancient urinations filled the compartment. The pharmacist held plastic-squeeze bottles joined with surgical tape. IV fluid from them came together at the charred remains of an enema nozzle.

"*¿Qué es?*" Art asked.

"Flame thrower," the Spaniard said. "Hypergolic rocket fuels work even in vacuum."

"What do you do when the nozzle melts?"

"Throw it before it explodes."

"Do you think it'll go through a THEM suit?"

"Do THEM wear suits?"

Art hadn't the foggiest idea. Had anyone ever seen a live THEM? The war had been going on for a long time and surely self-destruct programs couldn't always work perfectly. Probably somebody knew very well what THEM looked like. Perhaps they were so monstrous the news had been suppressed to prevent panic. Art fingered his alpenstock and wished he had some talent for improvising weapons. It looked as if he and Moonface were the only ones aboard without some ace in the hole. He gave a hollow laugh. They would never get within a half million kilometers of THEM before the *Nishrub* was vaporized like the rest of the Alliance fleet, so what was he worrying about? About being killed.

His ears popped again. He had his suit half closed before he realized it was only Bercovici coming back through the airlock. A moment later the stocky man came drifting past sick bay. He saw

Art. "Front tank split wide open," he said, "but that ice isn't going anywhere. No. Two'll pop any minute."

"*Grazzie.*" Art wondered what he had to be thankful about. As Bercovici pushed on toward the bridge the *Nishrub*'s straining hull shrieked again. By now he supposed ice was forming in No. 3. Suddenly Art had a horrible suspicion. He was halfway to the bridge when he realized the noncommittal Arab would tell him only when he was good and ready anyhow. Besides, why were they all sharpening alpenstocks and making weapons if . . .

Anyway, he had something else to worry about. The air scrubber was in a recess between No. 4 and the rearmost tanks. Once these froze it would be mashed, lines would rupture, and the *Nishrub* would be left with what air was now in the living quarters, plus the couple of hours' worth in their suits.

There was a loud crack and a hiss which ended sooner than he had expected. No. 2 was gone. Art wondered if it had frozen solid. If not, the *Nishrub* would be haloed with a kilometers-wide cloud of mist and vapor that even the laziest radarman could hardly fail to see. He wondered how far away the planetoid-sized THEM ship was by now.

"*Ahtt!*"

He sighed and pushed back toward the bridge.

"Berkóvich is busy," Jorf said. "Nobody else I trust."

Art remembered a bit of bullfighter slang: *Los huevos se me subieron hasta la garganta.* Art's testicles had not quite crawled up into his throat but he remembered various tasks in the Mediterranean which had been introduced with "nobody else I trust." But this time Jorf only wanted him to go outside and see if the holds were leaking.

Art checked his gear and turned up his suit heat. Moments later he was through the airlock and in the velvet darkness behind the rocky ice mass they had been tapping for water. He fired a gram-sec and still drifted the wrong way. Then he remembered they were firing. He held down the trigger of his thruster and finally started drifting toward the bow. From outside he could see what Jorf was up to.

Using the *Nishrub* like a tugboat, he was nudging the asteroid in the direction of THEM. Art wondered if their computers would be curious enough over the slight change in velocity to sound an alarm.

He bumped to a landing on the ice mass and hooked in with his alpenstock before he could bounce off. There was no water vapor around the *Nishrub*'s bow so he guessed No. 1 had frozen solid before the meter-wide crack had snaked down the capsule-shaped hull. He could not hear the creaks and groans but imagination supplied them as he saw the crack creep toward living quarters.

He began hooking his way toward the edge of the asteroid. It took a moment for his eyes to adjust and even then he almost missed the THEM ship. Squinting into the sun, he tried to determine if it was growing larger or smaller. No way.

He had never been outside while under way before. Things could get hairy if he missed the airlock and drifted into the ion exhaust. He played it safe and crawled down the hull. When he delivered his report Jorf was impassive. But the Arab had never been an ex-plainer. Art remembered when he had been picked up by the *guardia civil* in Spain.

It had all been complicated by Art's own ambivalent attitude. He had gone to Spain to see a brutal fascist dictatorship and that was exactly what he had seen. The laws were harsh and the police enforced them. When he strolled down a darkened street the *guardia civil* was there. When he camped on an isolated beach they appeared.

Where the poor lived in picturesque squalor he watched for the scowl or angry gesture at some *guardia's* back. It was not there. In some villages the *guardia* had the only concrete-floored square. Young people were not being dragged to the weekly dance there. Art had grown to like a country where people could walk down dark streets at night—where a stolen car made shocked headlines.

Which only increased his discomfort when the *guardia* picked him up that day. They did their job rather well, he thought, compared with the smarmy politeness he remembered in the States. They visited their friendly way about the village, playing with children, making life possible for that majority who wanted only to be left alone. And Jorf made a hobby of killing them.

Men, Art included, obeyed the grizzled Moor without question. This, Art supposed, was what the Greeks had meant by charisma. But he still didn't know what made Jorf Ali tick.

He did know that soon after he and Jorf's crew had been picked up, the *comandante* of the *guardia civil* had been exiled to the Canary Islands. He had wondered how the unpredictable Arab had

swung that. But there was no point in dissecting the dead remains of
Mediterranean politics. Probably the only nice thing about THEM
was that everybody knew exactly where he stood.

The crew crowded around Art eager for the latest word. He told
them what he had seen outside.

"Does it look just like ours?" a Japanese asked.

"Except that it's a few thousand times bigger."

"Still retro firing?"

"Too close to the sun for me to see."

"How soon will we come together?" a Brazilian persisted.

Art didn't know.

"Does the Old Man think they're gonna stand still while he pushes
a rock at them?" the pharmacist asked.

"Ask him," Art suggested. "Meanwhile, how about everybody
checking somebody else's air tanks?"

Four crewmen had loose valves and had already lost half their
air. While they were recharging Art tried to think of what else could
go wrong. Christ, what a laugh! They were heading for suicide. He
didn't know which frightened him the most: his imminent nonexistence, or the knowledge that two hundred men were watching him.
He really didn't care about the two hundred men, he decided. But
Jorf . . .

If the hunk of rock and ice came close enough to annoy THEM the
planet-sized ship would casually blow it to atoms. If the Alliance
fleet was any indication, the *Nishrub* would disappear in that same
instant, before he had a chance to brace himself. He'd say a prayer
or sing a death song if he knew any but Art had grown up in a society
affluent enough to do without these dubious comforts. Damn it, he
thought, all those good years thrown away! He wasn't just frightened.
He hoped the *Nishrub* would stay together long enough to do some
damage—scrape some paint, make those sons of bitches have to come
out and clean up the mess.

There was a clang-pop and the *Nishrub* shuddered.

"There goes No. 3," Art said. He supposed he ought to go out
again and see if they were losing water but before he could make up
his mind he saw Bercovici coming in. "Three forward holds frozen,"
the engineering officer said cheerfully.

Which meant the scrubber was already mashed or torn loose. There was an emergency air tank. The dial was calibrated in some Alliance measurement he had never been able to reconcile with PSI or kg/cm². Either way, they were breathing emergency air already and the dial was halfway down.

Jorf was standing behind him. "Plenty," he said. "What temperature No. 5?"

Without power there was only one way to find out. The eight-hundred meter passageway was rimed with hoarfrost. No. 4 was half frozen. No. 5 was only three-tenths of a degree above zero.

"Turn on heat in No. 5," Jorf said. "Tell crew use power again."

Blind unreasoning panic surged through Art. Jorf had been afraid to use power lest their position be revealed. They must be so close it no longer mattered. Any moment there would be searing heat, then the *Nishrub* and more especially Art would cease to exist. He switched on the PA and repeated the announcement in the languages he could remember. The hull shrieked. Jorf was looking at him. Art struggled to control himself. Abruptly the grizzled man said, "We talk now."

Art wondered what words of inspiration the Old Man would have before they all went out in a blaze of unchronicled glory. There was a moment's silence, then Jorf began speaking in careful Arabic. When he had finished Art began in English: "This is not suicide. We are going to live. Everybody turn suit heat all the way, go into No. 5. When you come out, kill."

As Art repeated the message the crew listened in silence, the more alert already rushing the portable airlock. Bercovici left the bridge. Art guessed he was going to open a hatch. Each tank had access at either end for maintenance when accelerating or retro firing without tons of water sloshing out the manhole. Art wondered what would happen to anyone submerged in near freezing water whose heater failed. He supposed he'd better get up there and make sure Moonface and a half dozen others had their suits buttoned up and heat on. He was moving when Jorf said, "Wait."

Art waited. He hadn't really believed this was going to happen. Smugglers didn't fight pitched battles against overwhelming odds. They "kept a low profile" as Nixon's Nitwits used to put it.

A scratchy voice came over the radio. *"Tutto pronto,"* Bercovici was saying. Art wondered how the engineer had gotten outside. His voice came louder and Art realized he must have been near the terminator taking bearings on THEM.

"Tell him come in."

The trilingual triestino was still cheerful when he entered the bridge, hoarfrost still sparkling on the metal parts of his suit. "Miss by hundred kilometers," he said.

This must be why they were still alive. The THEM was too large for evasive action but THEM's computers had predicted this harmless miss and ignored it.

Nessim and McQuoyd were hurrying men through the airlock. It would take forever. Art glanced at Jorf. The skipper nodded. "Everybody button up," Art said. "Tear that damn airlock off and get them moving."

The Belfast mate nodded and waved.

It still didn't make sense. Why send the crew into a half empty tank of water? Remembering how the Alliance fleet had blinked out one by one, it seemed to Art only to mean a brief scalding agony instead of instant incineration. He tried to console himself with the knowledge that at least he would have time to know he was dying.

The holo had come alive again, along with the heat, which was melting hoarfrost in the bridge. The *Nishrub* glowed green in the middle. Behind the sky was empty, save for the usual asteroidal garbage. The forward half of space was blanked out by the mass of rock they were pushing.

Half of the crew still waited to get through the opening. If he were ever to design his own spaceship, Art decided he was going to have one with larger doors. After months in zero grav even the few grams acceleration were enough to make the men clumsy. McQuoyd and Nessim had stationed themselves at each side of the hatchway and were literally throwing the crew through it. Art glanced back at the holo.

A faint pinkish halo was forming around the blankness that represented their rock-ice mass. Art reached for the fine tune but Jorf shook his head. THEM was filling so much of the sky that even at this angle their bit of asteroid was only partially eclipsing it.

"Hundred kilometer miss!" Art muttered. They were heading beyond terror now. He watched Jorf's fingers play over the key-straight toward THEM! The knowledge didn't frighten him. He was board. Arab script flicked on the screen faster than Art could read it.

Bercovici made an inquiring noise and the skipper repeated the readout in European script. Art still couldn't understand it but the engineering officer seemed satisfied. McQuoyd and Nessim were pitching crew as fast as they could but a distressingly large number still waited. Art was running a gloved finger over the sharpened edge of his alpenstock when he suddenly realized this was an excellent way to puncture his suit.

The pinkish halo was creeping from one edge of the rock mass, growing thick at the other. They weren't heading straight for THEM after all. Art glanced at the near-miss indicator but it gave only the zero distance to the rock-ice mass. Jorf glared at the hatchway as if will power could force the men through more quickly. Art heard the engineering officer mumble *"Archimedi."*

He tried to remember what Archimedes had done. Water—displacement, specific gravity—should have paid attention during those science courses . . . something about unborn babies suspended in amniotic fluid who managed to survive crashes that killed their mothers.

The pink mass was growing larger than the asteroid they shoved, overshadowing one half of it. Finally the last man was through. McQuoyd and Nessim dived after them. Jorf punched more instructions. "You still here?" he asked as he glanced up again. Art hastened toward the hatchway. There he hesitated. "Want me to dog it?"

"No." Jorf's voice came tinny through the suit radio. "Maybe we come out this way." They pushed against the infinitesimal acceleration and climbed into No. 5. "This one we close," Jorf said.

Art was helping dog it down when he felt a faint hesitation, the change so slight he didn't really know the *Nishrub* was retro firing until he saw an amorphous wall of water peppered with space-suited crew move gently toward him.

He felt the pressure but the cold didn't bother him. Water swirled gently, filled with trapped bubbles of—it couldn't be air. The hold had been open to the vacuum of space for nearly an hour. Cavitation, he guessed. Water did strange things under zero pressure and gravity. Crew bumped him in this whipped cream froth. Then things spun crazily.

He thought it was vertigo, then he knew the *Nishrub* was spinning on its own cg as attitude jets fired under Jorf's programming. The mass of water surged again. Art felt sudden squeezing pressure. Bubbles reabsorbed and the water began clearing. He caught shadowy glimpses of space-suited crew. Something about the weight distribution of their suits was making them all face the same way, like a school of sardines.

It was like diving. The *Nishrub* must be firing full-bore. Even underwater Art could feel the tug of gravity. His space suit was not rigged for neutral buoyancy. He was sinking toward the rear of the tank as the water cleared. Overhead he could see a clearly defined surface, just like on Earth.

The *Nishrub* must be moving like a bullet in passing gear, probably at right angles to its rock-ice cover. Art hoped they were using the asteroidal mass to conceal their getaway but, knowing Jorf, that was too much to hope. Otherwise, why would they all be underwater?

CHAPTER SIX

Art's suit was dragging him about the way the others pointed. He was more helpless than an individual in a shoal of fish for the space suit had no swim fins. His radio was on but the silence was unmarred by the slightest scratch of static. He supposed line-of-sight transmission was unsuited for underwater. Didn't submarines use long wave or some such?

He tried to concentrate. Jorf's instructions to come out killing were straightforward enough but inevitably Moonface and half a dozen others would smile and offer flowers. The result would be Nature's kindly way of culling them out of the gene pool—if there were any Earth genes left.

Art wondered what would happen. They might come together at a vaporizing thousands of kilometers per hour. They might drift together. But an eight-hundred-meter-long hull full of— So that was why Jorf had wanted the heat off! Ice could be as lethal as any blunt instrument. What would happen to a few sardines caught in the middle?

Bercovici had mumbled *"Archimedi."* Art remembered something about distributing G-stresses over the entire body surface, thus to escape being drawn and quartered by deceleration. He remembered far more vividly the brisk way Jorf had gotten out of the Mediterranean before that limpet mine went off. This was too close to dynamiting fish.

Art's faceplate turned milky. He felt a faint deceleration and wondered why they were retro firing. Water settled majestically against the forward bulkhead and began clearing again.

Abruptly Art knew what the deceleration meant. They had already hit! Christ, he thought, all that worry and we just *drifted* together! Later he would realize the retro firing had only been to bring the water and crew to the front end of the hold and position them for the

It was a frozen moment of total chaos. A shock wave passed through the aged waterboat as the ruptured bow forced its way into THEM amid magnificent clouds of cracked ice, fog, and a micro-second later—steam.

Art knew he had to get out soon but he was spinning in a whirlpool. In an instant of kaleidoscopic vision he saw the hatch but he was being swept away from it. Something struck him between the legs and he grabbed frantically. It was his alpenstock. Shrieks and groans of yielding metal punctuated the gurgle of flowing water. Above it all was a sustained shriek-roar like a jet taking off. In a moment he would know what THEM looked like. He had no choice. Water was cascading from a rent in the hull, sweeping him and two hundred other men into whatever they had hit.

There were scratchy noises as his radio started working again. He slammed into a bulkhead and doubled, gasping for breath. Men slammed blindly into him. Some untouched corner of his mind won-dered if THEM had artificial gravity. *Something* was making water gush out of the *Nishrub* with the exuberance of a Norwegian waterfall.

There were more bumps and thumps before the stream lost its force. He was on hands and knees in something like normal Earth gravity, looking back past the *Nishrub*'s bulk down an untidy two-hundred-meter-wide tunnel through smashed and twisted metal. It looked as if they had penetrated several kilometers before coming to rest.

The constant whistling roar was air leaking out of this rent. Mixed in the turbulent stream was water from the tank he had just exited. He was hot. He switched off his suit and still heat poured through the insulated fabric. Forward, where the *Nishrub*'s frozen bow tanks had borne the brunt of penetration, was a jumble of cracked ice which had reacted with THEM's warm atmosphere to produce fog. Then, as outrushing air brought the cloud toward him, Art saw it was steam created when kinetic energy had been abruptly transformed into heat. A scalded body in scarlet trousers floated by.

Art had known the THEM ship was big but from outside he had not been able to imagine—it must be like living in a hollow planet. Emptied of her water cargo, the *Nishrub* could have carried a hundred thousand people in reasonable comfort. But the *Nishrub* had gone into THEM like a small caliber bullet into a whale, save that from all the hissing and shrieking the *Nishrub* must have penetrated past the blubber.

More bodies floated by, each wearing the same scarlet trousers. Art wondered what had stripped off their space suits without removing this odd garment. The bodies were so scalded he couldn't recognize them. He shuddered. A moment ago there had been a veritable welter of bodies tumbling out of the split hull. Now he seemed to be the only one left. He looked around the gap between twisted girders and the scarred flank of the *Nishrub*.

"*Ahtt!*" The sound rang tinny in his radio.

Art was so relieved he almost cried. "*Ahna hénnah!*" he yelled. "I'm here; where are you?"

"Forward," Jorf said. "Say everybody, 'Get you ass up here.'"

Art rang the linguistic changes as he struggled forward against the flow of air and steam. It was getting hotter. Sweat ran down his face and the glass began to fog. He rubbed his gloved hand over it but the fog was on the inside. So far he hadn't seen any THEM. He wondered if there were any. Maybe they stayed home and conducted their wars by remote control. That would explain their incredible no-surrender bravery. Maybe they *were* the ship instead of riding inside it. Maybe . . . It was getting ungodly hot. How much longer was his air good for?

Air still leaked out the hole the *Nishrub* had punched. Did THEM breathe air? They must or why keep such a dangerous and corrosive substance aboard? But was this gas air? He could open his faceplate and find out but Art thought it prudent to let someone else perform that experiment first.

"*Ahtt!* Tell them sons of backward-pissing camels hurry up!"

Art did. "Where are you?" he repeated. "I can't see anything."

"*ĀH-lah tool!*" Jorf yelled, *straight ahead,* and added phrases Art had only heard on occasions when grammar lessons were inadvisable.

He became aware of prayers and death songs as men struggled to assemble. He blew against his faceplate and twiddled the windshield wiper gadget that was supposed to keep the inside clean. Finally he saw twisted evidence of the *Nishrub*'s entry between wisps of steam.

A crewman appeared. Art grabbed his arm. The man swung his alpenstock and punctured the space where Art's head had recently been, then recognized him. *"Entschuldigen Sie bitte,"* the blue-eyed man said. It was the first time Art had ever heard him admit knowing German.

"Ahtt! feyn éntah?"

"I know where I am," Art snapped. "Where the hell are you?" They struggled against the wind. Would this ship never run out of air? Surely there were hatches for damage control. How big a section had they holed? But air escaped unabated as he and the blue-eyed man slogged forward over girders, struggling against a gravity that seemed occasionally to waver and shift direction. Finally they saw another space-suited man, walking the wrong way.

That'll be Moonface, Art decided. He was struggling to intercept him when abruptly the other turned and began walking the right way. Jorf's voice was getting louder. Finally Art saw him.

The man who had been going the wrong way had lost his alpenstock. He held something that had a loop antenna sticking out of one side. When Jorf yelled *"Ahtt!"* again the man without an alpenstock pocketed his gadget and began walking toward the captain.

He was moving oddly, almost as if he wanted to stay out of Jorf's sight. Art wondered if Moonface had lost what little mind he had. The man beside Art held a gloved finger before his faceplate. He took Art's arm and they crept silently over the wreckage. Moonface was within three meters of Jorf's back. He held something in his hand. "Hey!" Art yelled.

When Moonface spun and pointed the odd-shaped thing at him Art suspected he had been imprudent. The German began moving cautiously. Jorf spun. Without hesitation he threw his alpenstock. The butt end struck Moonface in the small of the back. Instantly the blue-eyed man jumped.

"Don't hurt him!" Art yelled. "He's a little on the stupid side."

But the German's pick swung in a vicious arc. Air and pink foam gushed from the suit.

"You didn't have to kill him!" Art wailed.

"Didn't I?" the German asked.

Art looked into the faceplate. It was not Moonface. He had never seen the man before. He wished he hadn't called Moonface stupid.

Men clustered, babbling questions.

"Quiet!" Jorf roared. "Everybody got alpenstock?"

There were murmurs of assent. "Anyone doesn't have one?" Art asked in the usual languages. When there was no answer Jorf added, "You see anybody without, you kill."

Art wondered if THEM— The face inside the space suit looked human. Was he a slave, a POW, some *Nishrub* man Art hadn't recognized? Art had a feeling that something was horribly wrong.

He didn't have time to formulate his doubts. Abruptly the roar of escaping air lessened, puffed once more for an instant, then ceased to a whisper. In the sudden silence Art could hear men's breathing over the radio. Suddenly it was darker in the gap between the *Nishrub* and the wall of THEM wreckage.

Something was unrolling behind them to seal off the hole. He wondered if it was automatic, then saw tiny space-suited figures working around the edges. Jorf began walking, swaying like a diver bucking bottom currents as the gravity wavered.

Jorf would want him close. Art pushed his way through the mass of silent men until he could touch Jorf on the shoulder. The grizzled Arab spun and grinned. Unlike Art, he was having fun.

The space-suited figures working with the patch paid no attention. Art wondered if they were human. Maybe they had totally different senses and couldn't see. But the space suits were human-shaped. As they came closer he saw they were practically the same as those worn by the *Nishrub*'s men. He was trying to figure how to break this news to Jorf without using the radio when the Arab yelled, "Now!"

Definitely, Art was in the wrong place. He wondered if Vietnam had been anything like this. Jorf led and Art was nearly crushed in the rush to follow. The figures patching the leak turned in surprise as humans swarmed over them swinging alpenstocks. Each time a pick penetrated a space suit pink foam jetted out with the escaping air. To Art it looked just like the blood that had come from the stranger who had . . . this repair party couldn't be THEM. He was pushed into the thick of it and suddenly came face to face with one. That was a

man—a human being inside that suit. He looked European. He swung
something at Art. It looked like a wrench.

My God, Art thought, he's trying to kill me! He didn't know why
the idea was so startling. The tool hurt as it came down on his shoulder. Art swung his alpenstock and missed. He jabbed with the handle
but the other man was swinging again. This time Art caught him in
the faceplate with the chisel end of his climbing tool. Blood, air,
and shattered glass shot forward and spattered Art's own faceplate. He
wiped and it smeared. Through the red haze he saw another space-
suited figure in front of him.

Art swung again. As bloody foam spouted some corner of his
mind evolved a tortuous kindergarten logic: I've hurt two of these
guys. They're going to be plenty mad. I can't stop now.

The rest of the *Nishrub*'s crew seemed to be undergoing no crisis
of conscience. He heard shouts, grunts, happy excited laughter.
Strange space-suited figures kept appearing before his red-fogged
faceplate, almost like cattle in a slaughterhouse. Art wondered if
killing was always this easy. He was swinging wildly now, whacking
at anything that didn't have a tool like his own. Suddenly it was over.

He swayed, catching his breath, and finally his hand was steady
enough to wipe the mess from his faceplate. The strangers were still
oozing bubbly messes from punctured suits. Their patch had covered
the greater part of the gap left by the *Nishrub* but air was still leaking.
Bercovici appeared. "Should we finish the job?"

It took a moment to realize the engineer meant the patch and not
the rest of THEM. Jorf waved his hand in a negative gesture. *"We*
got suits," he said.

A man climbed down from twisted girders near where the patch
was secured. *"Compuertas,"* he said, and Art recognized the pharmacist. "Manhole up there," Art interpreted, then remembered Jorf
knew Spanish.

Jorf was still in front and Art couldn't very well stay behind. He
had just killed several people. What would happen if he were to
vomit inside a space suit? The realization that the next stranger
might kill him was not helping to settle his stomach. He was tired and
beginning to ache. He wished THEM's gravity would either settle
down or stop entirely. These bewildering shifts of direction were
harder on his stomach than a guilty conscience.

The manhole went from one internal part of the ship to another and had no airlock. Art and Jorf were struggling with it when Bercovici pushed them aside. He stuck a gloved finger in an unexpected place and the latch moved. The door slammed violently outward but the engineering officer had been standing to one side. They pushed against the outrushing air.

Art caught a glimpse of men standing before panels of dials and switches. Abruptly they rushed for emergency lockers. Some actually made it. Others fell, blood pouring from mouths and noses as they gasped their airless lives away. The *Nishrub*'s men poured through the hatchway.

Those THEM still alive struggled with emergency canisters. One man ripped his off and threw it. Art drove his pick into a yielding skull. This didn't seem right but Art didn't have time to think about it. There was something horribly wrong about all of this.

He wondered if they had made a mistake and were attacking one of the Alliance's own ships. But he remembered the Friend-or-Foe identification. He had seen the Alliance fleet flicker into nonexistence on the holo. These sons of bitches had probably destroyed Earth by now. He drove his alpenstock into another violet-haired skull. Blood and brains spouted satisfyingly as he wrenched his pick loose and sought another victim. These human-appearing monsters had destroyed Earth and the entire Alliance fleet. Now several THEM seemed hell-bent on destroying him! Art gouged a bubbling furrow in another head. An ear came off and hung like a neatly spindled trophy. He wanted to get rid of it but they had forced THEM into a corner. The twenty who still lived fought desperately. Art was in front and with so many men behind him there was no way not to stay there. He swung at another skull and missed. Blood spurted from a THEM's shoulder.

The half-dozen THEM still alive raised their hands. Art hesitated but there was no stopping the others. Seconds later the last corpse was foaming blood in the airless compartment. *Nishrub* men were struggling to open the next compartment.

Suddenly it opened. Men in space suits came out propelled by the air behind them. Art expected firearms or something Buck Rogerish but each suited stranger carried a basket-gripped rapier. They looked clumsy.

One thrust at Art. He smashed at the other's faceplate an instant before the rapier tip touched him. As electricity stiffened him, Art understood why the rapier cattle prod was thicker than it had to be. In the moment it took to recover he saw Jorf take a stab of electricity in his left arm. The stranger was thrusting again when Art's alpenstock changed his plans. Jorf shook himself and was whole again. *We're quits,* Art thought. *He saved my life; I saved his.*

He wondered if they shouldn't take prisoners for interrogation but the *Nishrub*'s men had all come from Earth. There was no more stopping them now than arguing with feeding sharks.

There was a delighted crowing over the radio. A man produced a submachine gun that looked as if it had been manufactured on Earth. Moments later every *Nishrub* man had one. To Art's consternation the man who had found the guns was Moonface.

The next manhole was so large not even bullets could budge it. A machinist dragged up a welding cylinder. He started to warn people away but the crew were already putting metal between themselves and the doorway. Art had heard of the possibilities when oxygen and acetylene were mixed. He supposed there would be a gratifying pop.

Even in the vacuum the explosion felt like the end of the world. The ends of the steel cylinder departed, tearing gaps in bulkheads at either end of the compartment. The main part of the cylinder parted down the welded seam. Centimeter-thick steel unrolled and lay flat against the door. The door came from its hinges and sailed across the compartment in majestic slow motion. They poured through and started killing again.

There was something horribly wrong. Art needed to sit down and figure things out. But nobody seemed inclined to give him the time. The human-appearing strangers seemed to be trying to surrender. At least Art guessed that was what their odd way of crossing empty hands over their breasts must mean. He killed another one and during a momentary lull checked the corpse for hidden weapons. He wouldn't know a THEM weapon if it bit him. Across the compartment a THEM crossed hands over his chest. A *Nishrub* man slung a piece of scrap iron and the man went down.

"Captain," Art gasped, "shouldn't we take some prisoners?"

Jorf sprayed bullets at three THEM who came through a hatchway carrying what looked like a sheet. "Sure," he said, and continued shooting.

Art wondered how long they could keep it up. This ship . . . there might be a million aboard. And women? If every man killed until he was exhausted they could hardly . . . Bercovici was struggling with a door which should open the opposite way. The machinist pushed it open a crack and shoved an oxygen cylinder through. A second later the door bulged outward. When Art looked in he saw this compartment was already mopped up.

Something was wrong with the next bomb. While the machinist was fixing it men tossed flaming bottles of the pharmacist's medicinal alcohol through the next opening. How many compartments would there be in a planet-sized ship? Most of the ship, Art supposed, would be for machinery, stores, armament. Some lucky fluke had put the *Nishrub* into a populated section. They had to be near the stern. The compartments they had smashed their bloody way through so far had all contained machinery and technicians.

The odd part was many THEM seemed surprised. Had any alarm been given? Perhaps the *Nishrub*'s kilometers-deep hole was so unimportant that THEM had not bothered to sound a General Quarters. Too damn many things just didn't seem right. They had found weapons, but no more than in an average city this size. But then, in a war where enemies vaporized each other from half the width of a solar system . . . Art supposed an aircraft carrier would be equally nonplussed if called upon to repel boarders.

The people he had seen so far had odd hair colors but they were no farther out than the Alliance's training officers. Non-Earth surely, but nonhuman?

POWs, slaves? Surely the no-surrender THEM would put up a better fight once the *Nishrub*'s people got to some important part of the ship. How many hundred kilometers would that be? When would the *Nishrub*'s people get a chance to sleep? Cortez must have had problems like this when his two hundred hungry men took on fifteen million. He had pulled it off by convincing the disaffected Indians that they'd be better off with him than under the heart-devouring Aztecs.

The door swung open and greasy smoke puffed out with the remains of the air. Singed corpses still sat at a table. It was unbelievable as a painting by Hieronymus Bosch. Art stared, trying to ignore the two-toned THEM thumpings that formed a constant background to the grunts and breathings of *Nishrub* radio. He wondered if THEM could hear him. Could they understand Earth languages? There was something oddly evocative about the high tone, low tone thumpings, as if he had heard it somewhere. Code, he guessed. How hard would it be to break? Jorf laughed.

"We ought to take some prisoners," Art insisted.

"Yah, sure." Jorf sprayed bullets through still another doorway. A man in emergency breathing gear cowered in a corner, hands over his chest. Jorf shot him. Art groaned.

While he was trying to explain the value of live prisoners another door opened and a man pointed what looked like a camera with a telephoto lens. Art had a sickening suspicion that he was not going to take a picture. They spun toward the new menace but at that moment a hammerhead and a broken stump of handle whizzed past them and drove lens splinters back up the tube. The "camera" glowed, then became a blazing miniature sun. In the instant before the THEM collapsed Art saw both of his hands had burned off.

It was all very odd. Even this cameralike heat gun didn't look like a weapon. Probably it was some sort of tool just like the *Nishrub*'s welding bottles and rescue saws. There was an air of desperate improvisation—as if THEM had never expected combat. Could this be the wrong ship?

The *Nishrub*'s men were already surging into the next compartment. There had to be a companionway somewhere. Passing from hole to hole they could take centuries and meanwhile—how long had they been at it now? Not long enough for his air to run out. But sooner or later THEM would recover from their initial shock—or get around to spraying some insecticide.

There was a booming voice like the wrath of a vengeful god. After a moment Art realized he was hearing it through bone conduction or some such, transmitted into the airless compartment through the ship's structure and via his feet. "Throw down your weapons," the voice said in English. "You've proved yourselves. We do not kill brave men."

"We do," Jorf said. He wrestled with a latch.

CHAPTER SEVEN

"Somebody knows we're here," Art muttered.

As they plowed through the next compartment Art noticed subtle changes. Had he been military-minded he would have decided they were entering officers' country. Suddenly he realized the significance of the booming voice. "Getting close to the bridge," he told Jorf.

"I know," the Arab grinned.

A bulkhead slid smoothly up like a curtain before them. Behind it a dozen THEM in space suits stood poised with telephoto-camera gadgets.

"Ahlah tool!" Jorf yelled. Beside him a man suddenly doubled, a smoking half-meter gap in his midsection. The others swarmed forward. Heat guns flashed once and when they didn't repeat Art guessed they needed a second to recharge, just like a camera strobe light. The unfortunate technicians had all been alpenscragged before they were ready for a second shot.

They *are* improvising. Nothing that slow and clumsy could be designed as a weapon. But he had seen three *Nishrub* men die. How many skirmishes could they win before there were no *Nishrub* people left? "Ought to take some prisoners," he repeated.

"Yeah," Jorf agreed. "Maybe you right." He opened the next compartment. Men stared from open shower stalls and Art bemusedly noted each had pubic hair in the same violet or purple to match his head. He wondered if the color was natural or just a meticulous attention to style. THEM must have very odd social customs. The men stepped dazedly from shower stalls and still dripping crossed palms over their naked chests. They were still breathing—and without suits! Somewhere in their bloody progress a hatch had been dogged behind them. Air pressure could only mean THEM were now behind them cleaning up the damage.

The Arab grunted. Art stared, remembering THEM's no-surrender reputation. The THEM who had been showering a moment ago were now gasping, collapsing, dying. One snatched an emergency canister from a bulkhead but he died before he could get it over his head.

"All right already! We surrender."

The booming voice was amused. Art was wondering how Jorf would react when the grizzled Arab said, "Bring me captain."

They waited. There was a warning hum and the voice came again. "We are entering by the opposite doorway. Please remember, we surrender."

"So did they," Jorf muttered, with a glance at the naked bodies in front of him.

The door opened and their captain entered. He was medium tall and human-appearing, save for shoulder-length violet hair. His uniform was a compendium of every comic opera banana dictatorship Art had ever seen or imagined. Epaulets extended winglike beyond his shoulders. His blue and orange tunic sagged with gold braid. Medals crossed his chest and tangled with the ribbon that hung from his neck. He wore a sword.

Jorf emptied half a clip of ammo into him. "Now send me your real captain," he growled when he had finished mowing down the escort. He waited a second for a reply. He was reaching for the latch to the next doorway when abruptly he stopped. The latch was turning.

The Spanish pharmacist positioned himself. As the door flew open he squeezed his enema apparatus. Hypergolic fuel flared and spattered around the doorway but most of it went through into the next compartment. The Spaniard flung his flame thrower into the blazing doorway and jumped aside. There was a whoosh-crump. They waited for the fire to burn out.

Bercovici unlatched the next door. This compartment was a lounge, several cuts more luxurious. Getting warm, Art guessed. The lounge was empty. He remembered the seemingly solid bulkhead that had lifted. How many more surprises would this ship have? A man caught his sleeve.

Art looked into Moonface's idiotic grin. The singer of obscene songs grinned more widely and pulled. "What is it?" Art snapped. The broad face beamed blissfully and Moonface pulled harder. Art let himself be led to one side of the lounge. Moonface pointed at a large blank wall. "Yeah, so what?" Art asked.

Moonface did something with his feet and the wall became a bewildering tracery of green, yellow, black. For a moment it reminded Art of a loofah sponge, then abruptly he knew what this capsule-shaped tracery of an involuted circulatory system had to be. "Jorf!" he yelled, "this guy's found us a map of the ship!"

Jorf posted guards and came to study it. Once Art had caught his mental breath the diagram was self-explanatory. There was even a pulsating pink spot which could only mean "you are here."

Moonface had been shouldered aside in the rush. Art gave his happy idiotic face a sidelong glance. Moonface had contributed more to the success of this raid than he had. He caught the dark man's arm. "Show me how you turn it on."

Moonface led him to a spot where the deck was textured like a doormat. Sonofabitch! Art had been walking over these patches all around the ship. Moonface shuffled his feet on the mat. Abruptly the map disappeared from the bulkhead. Jorf said a single savage word in Arabic.

"Forget it," Art said. "Let's move."

Jorf gave him an odd look, then moved at right angles to their previous blind course. The next compartment was empty. This seemed faintly ominous to Art but he saw another odd patch of flooring. He shuffled his foot and another bulkhead came alive with a schematic of the ship's endless kilometers of corridors.

"We surrender," the wrathful god voice boomed again.

Art looked at Jorf. The grizzled Arab was impassive. There was a moment of tense silence.

"What proof do you wish of our sincerity?" the voice boomed.

Jorf made a sound like rotten canvas tearing. Art searched for a polite way to say it. He wished he could wipe his sweating face but he was still inside a space suit. "Can you hear me?" he asked over the suit radio.

"We hear you."

"As collateral my captain desires your collective cullions, sliced thin with a rusty knife, and curried." Remembering what had happened to the Alliance fleet, Art decided Jorf's demand was reasonable.

There was no answer.

The grizzled Arab went back to the map Moonface had conjured out of another bulkhead. Finally he grunted. It took Art a while to see what Jorf had seen. They were traveling almost parallel with a companionway—a main artery, but a couple of levels above it.

Bercovici studied the diagram and scratched his head. Their passage had been through repair manholes. The trouble was, there were no manholes up or down. McQuoyd and Nessim muttered but offered no suggestions. Art looked despairingly about the compartment. Abruptly he stared. A hole gaped in the deck in front of Moonface.

Going down it, Art felt another of those odd gravitic waverings and suddenly *he* was level and the men behind him were sideways. Jorf pushed ahead of him and stepped onto a moving beltway. Though Art followed him on without difficulty the walls were now blurring with speed. He looked back and saw all the *Nishrub*'s people were boarding.

Jorf was counting fingers and muttering. He stepped to the edge and the beltway slowed. They branched into a narrower corridor and slowed still more. "This time maybe we take prisoner," he growled. Art interpreted, wondering if anyone would remember.

Bercovici and McQuoyd forced the door. Art held his breath but this time nobody threw homemade weapons. Finally Nessim looked cautiously through it. He stared a moment, then went in.

The space suit helped preserve the illusion, Art supposed. If he'd been able to sniff whatever the attendant was offering, it probably wouldn't smell like coffee. The violet-haired man was polishing his machine and gave no more than a cursory glance to the space-suited invaders. Obviously they weren't officers, nor did they want whatever came from his hot drink dispenser. McQuoyd grabbed him. There was a moment's confusion as the mate searched for something to tie him. Finally he gave up. Herding the bewildered messman in front, they passed through the next doorway.

"Jackpot!" Art muttered.

The holo was logarithmically larger than the one in the *Nishrub*'s bridge. Instruments whose use Art could only guess at lined the bulkheads of the immense command center. Rows of consoles, each with its own holo screen, were vaguely reminiscent of that control center somewhere in Texas. A hundred men stood rigid, each with empty palms crossed before his chest.

"Who is captain?" Jorf growled.

"Are you through killing for a while?" It was the same booming voice that had called on them to surrender.

Art could not tell which of the prisoners had spoken. He glanced worriedly at Jorf but he couldn't see his face inside the suit. Not that a suit made any difference. Art had never been able to tell what the grizzled Arab was thinking. He took a calculated risk and said, "If the commander will step forward and answer questions possibly a surrender can be arranged."

There was a moment's silence. The hundred-man staff stood rigid, palms crossed before their chests. Art held his breath. Any second now Jorf would lose patience and begin shooting. Finally there was movement. The messman who had been cleaning his hot drink machine turned to face Jorf. "I am the captain," he said. "Now, if you're through with your amok or whatever it's called, perhaps we can discuss terms."

Jorf made a sound like a gear box starting to seize up. Art translated without embellishment: "Me everything, you nothing."

"Very well," the captain smiled. "Shall we get down to details?"

Art began interpreting but Jorf seemed to be understanding without difficulty. "Tell everybody surrender," the Arab said. "Bring all arms. One of my men is hurt, everybody die."

"Succinct and unmistakable," the THEM commander said. "May my staff be allowed to transmit the message?"

Jorf nodded.

The THEM captain hesitated. "Is that an affirmative?"

Art said it was and very slowly two of the men standing with crossed palms returned to their consoles.

"How many men aboard?" Art asked.

"About five thousand."

Jorf snorted. "Ask about women, children, animals."

"They are included in the previous figure."

"Hah!" Jorf snarled, "Also you speak Arabic?"

"Not exactly," the THEM captain said good-humoredly. "But our computers do."

To Art it seemed as if the booming voice was speaking the same classic Arabic he had heard over Mediterranean radio whenever the Egyptians got into a pan-Islamic mood long enough to soften their g's. Now that he was standing still for a moment he had time to realize how hot and sticky this space suit was becoming.

"Cover me," Jorf growled, and walked across to one of the staff still standing with crossed palms. He tilted the unresisting man's head back and looked up his nostrils, then forced his mouth open. He beckoned to the Spanish pharmacist. They muttered together for a moment and finally Art realized Jorf could guess considerably more about advanced technology than he had suspected. The captain did not resist when Jorf and the pharmacist examined him in the same way. Finally satisfied that the THEM had no miniature gas masks or other implanted equipment, the grizzled Arab asked, "You breathe Earth air?"

"Not exactly." To Art it seemed that the spurious messman had not stopped laughing at them.

A *Nishrub* man made a strangling sound, clearly audible over suit radio. He was tearing open his faceplate. They watched tensely. Art wondered how much air was left in his own bottles. The THEM captain was explaining that humanoids from every part of the universe breathed each other's air without difficulty when Art felt the warning flutter that meant his own air was giving out. The other *Nishrub* man was still alive. Art guessed he had little choice.

After a shocked moment he decided the air was breathable. He had breathed city air. He had breathed country air, clean salt sea air. But he had never breathed anything like this profusion of unidentifiable smells and quasi stinks. Not that they were offensive—but they were certainly *different*.

There was a faint hint of cumin and saffron, and other spices common to Arab cooking, overlaid with an even more vague suggestion of the acrid camel stink that permeates every Moroccan town. There was a smell he associated with flowers, though he hadn't the faintest idea what kind. Jorf opened his faceplate and after one startled look his gaze became once more hooded.

Art wondered if this was part of some psychological game to put Arab-speakers off guard. Vaguely he remembered reading somewhere that smell was the sense most intimately connected with the emotions. He wanted to warn Jorf, but the Arab seemed in no need of admonitions.

"How many living organisms aboard?" Art asked suddenly.

The captain frowned and turned to the men still standing with crossed palms behind him. One spoke briefly in a language Art had never heard. The captain turned back. "Approximately one million times ten to the millionth."

"A minute ago he said five thousand," Jorf muttered.

"Men," the THEM captain corrected. "Living organisms must include everything."

"You got that many women?"

"He may be counting the yeast cells in the bakery," Art contributed.

"Naturally," the captain smiled. "Also in the wine cellars, breweries, and recycling vats. Then there are the E coli in every intestinal tract, the meningococci which lurk always ready to pounce on any uninoculated humanoid. And no doubt you've just introduced a few choice specimens of your own to plague those of us who remain alive."

"How many organisms with an intelligence equal or superior to our own?" Art probed. *A real clown,* he grumbled to himself when he caught the THEM captain's look of sly amusement. Jorf growled and fondled his alpenstock.

"There were five thousand men aboard," the THEM commander sighed. "No bug-eyed monsters, no women. Only men like you and me."

"This ship could carry millions!" Art protested.

"I do not carry passengers. And surely you don't think we stoke combustibles or take in sail or whatever it is you do by hand?"

"How do you run this ship?" Art asked.

"Until you damaged some controls and then killed every technician sent to repair them, I did it by issuing the proper orders. Now . . ." The commander shrugged.

"Won't it run at all?"

"I haven't had time to find out."

McQuoyd turned to Jorf. "This ship was pretty close to the center of the fleet," he said. "And if memory serves me, no THEM was damaged."

"I know," Jorf growled without changing expression.

In the excitement it had slipped Art's mind completely. Now he remembered they held only one ship in the midst of an unharmed fleet. Jorf didn't seem worried. But Art had never seen him worried. THEM had a reputation for no surrender. Art wondered if the rest of the fleet would turn on this ship once they knew it had surrendered. He wished he knew a way to warn Jorf but this damned alien seemed to understand every language.

Jorf was ignoring Art, speaking Arabic now. "Do the ship's weapons still work?"

The THEM commander nodded with a typically human gesture. "Will your fleet shoot at us?"

The alien laughed. "I'm afraid our bloodthirsty reputation has been somewhat enhanced by our enemies." He sighed. "What do you actually know about us?"

Art began wondering what kind of a con job the Alliance ambassador had pulled on Earth. Jorf's next remark pulled him back to reality. "You destroyed our fleet and our world," the Arab said. "Isn't that enough for us to enjoy killing you slowly?"

The alien was either very brave or very stupid. He laughed again. "Of course it is. But no, our companions will not shoot at us."

"Why?"

"This ship is larger than the others, has more communications equipment, and is strategically placed in the exact center of the fleet. I point out these things to avoid a long and tiresome interrogation."

"Hah." Jorf didn't sound surprised.

My God, Art thought, *the flagship!*

CHAPTER EIGHT

"Will they surrender?" Jorf asked.

"That was implicit with my own surrender. Without communications the fleet becomes disorganized."

Jorf was already at the holo. Its controls were basically the same as the *Nishrub*'s but with so many refinements that he was having trouble. "If you will permit me," the alien said.

It was true. The fleet spread a quarter astronomical unit in every direction. Each image was bright and clear without the fuzzy outlines of ion propulsion. "We've won!" Art said in sudden jubilation. Then he wondered what they had won. They had conquered THEM but was there any Earth left?

The *Nishrub*'s men were beginning to relax. Bercovici hovered over the console where a THEM staffer was relaying Jorf's surrender order over the intercom. Jorf glanced at him and snapped a single sharp word.

As they put distance between themselves and prisoners and checked weapons Art realized it was not going to be that easy. They had taken the flagship but there had only been two hundred *Nishrub* men at the beginning. Now there were a hundred-fifty. How long could they hold this immense ship, much less the fleet?

Jorf and the alien commander still conferred over the holo. Art turned to one of the rigid THEM still standing with crossed palms. "Do you understand me?"

"Yes." There was tolerant amusement in the violet-haired humanoid's answer.

"Were you drafted or did you volunteer?"

"We are all volunteers."

Art frowned. Technically he too had been a volunteer. "You look amazingly like the Alliance ambassador," he said. The only real difference seemed to be clothing. Everybody aboard this ship wore combination boots and trousers peg-topped to just under their hairless armpits. He wondered if THEM had ever invented shirts.

The staff officer smiled. "The human body is most suitable for tool handling. It crops up throughout the universe."

"Have you ever seen—" Hastily Art amended his question. "Do you know of any intelligent nonhuman life forms?"

"Many. Have you none on your own planet?"

It took Art a moment to see what he meant. Either this alien was extremely literal-minded or he was deriving his own quiet amusement from this interrogation. "I mean of equal or superior intelligence," Art said. "We can exclude the pigs and chickens."

"In that sense of the word there are none."

Art sighed. So THEM were human. It figured. Professional breast beaters were always insisting there was nothing more viciously destructive than a civilized human. These strangers seemed ultracivilized. But they were also far better off than Earth. "Why?" Art asked. "You don't need raw materials, you're not interested in bringing us the benefits of your civilization. We weren't big enough to be any danger to you. Why did you attack us?"

"Why do you attack mice?"

"They annoy us and destroy our food supplies. Were we annoying you?"

The alien did not answer. Art wondered why he seemed amused.

Everything he knew about THEM, Art realized, had come via their enemy. The Alliance ambassador had sucked Earth into this— "Is this some kind of private quarrel—a civil war?"

"You might call it that."

Either the alien's culture covered every unpleasant potentiality with a laugh—or this alien was truly and vastly amused. Art tried not to lose his temper. The rigid man in front of him must know how the *Nishrub*'s people had carved their way through the ship. He wondered if killing this one would encourage less evasive answers from the others.

"How do you make this ship move?"

"It has been damaged."

"How badly?"

"I do not have the technical knowledge to answer that."

"Who does?"

"Unfortunately, you seem to have killed them all."

Art wondered how his IQ stacked up with the average THEM's. Abruptly he wished he had been more patient with Moonface. He went back where Jorf and the alien commander studied the holo. "They will obey?" Jorf was asking.

"Unquestioningly," the alien replied in elegantly classic Arabic.

"Where are the people aboard this ship?"

The THEM commander snapped a question at the staffer manning a console. Art tried to separate a word out of the other's quick answer. It was as meaningless as the tonalities from THEM radio. How long would it take him to learn the language? Then he remembered.

"They are assembling in the crew's quarters," the alien commander said. "Do you wish to inspect?"

Art wasn't anxious to interrupt but . . . He took a deep breath. "First," he suggested, "could you patch us in on that translator of yours? I'd like to know what's going on and perhaps my captain would too."

Jorf was giving Art a level look of appraisal as the THEM commander gave orders. One of the staff cautiously uncrossed his palms and began moving. A moment later he returned with an armload of miniature headsets.

"I don't see any of you wearing these things," Jorf said.

"Ours are in our hairpieces."

"Then that violet color isn't natural?" Art asked.

"You think I have time to grow real hair?" the commander sniffed.

Art put an earphone cautiously to his head. "Say something."

"Power pollutes. The ratio of corruption is a function of technology versus cultural lag."

Art took the headset away and the alien's voice became unintelligible tonalities. He nodded and Jorf put on the set he had been examining for poisoned needles and other diabolical devices.

It wasn't until nearly a minute later that full realization of what this machine could mean finally soaked into Art. *I'm free! Now he doesn't need an interpreter. Never again will that anti-semitic Semite shout me awake in the midst of a dream of debauchery!* Jorf and the THEM commander were leaving to inspect the remainder of the crew. They did not look back for Art.

Art worried. It was nice to be free of those eternal shouts but he, Jorf, all the *Nishrub*'s people were in this together. And there was something very wrong about it all. Art couldn't guess what it was but that quiet amusement reminded him of some grandfather allowing himself to be "captured" by his bear-hunting descendants. Despite all the blood they had waded through getting to this ship's bridge, THEM were not taking them seriously. Were they of the same race? Were the THEM they had killed even alive? Maybe they were decoys cunningly done up to spout blood.

There was a tinny yammering in his radio. Art supposed he ought to take the suit off. He was out of air and had the faceplate open anyhow but . . . He turned back to the staff man he had been interrogating. "Where can I recharge my tanks?"

The THEM pointed to an emergency connection. Art was mildly astonished when his suit connection screwed into the outlet. He remembered the theory that THEM had been a race of planetbound primitives who had captured an Alliance ship. That would explain the similarities in minor details like thread gauges. He had finished filling his tanks before another unpleasant possibility occurred to him. "Here," he told the THEM. "You take a few deep breaths first."

The THEM made no effort to conceal his amusement as he complied. Finally Art was convinced. If they lost pressure, he was set for another two hours. The rest of the *Nishrub*'s crew was already following his example.

Art was turning off the suit radio's faint yammer when he realized who was talking. "Are you suggesting we should join forces against the Alliance?" The voice was Jorf's but the inflections were elegantly classical with no hint of the odd pronunciations or Berber phrases that peppered his Moroccan dialect.

"Any decision must be your own," the THEM commander replied. "I shall have discharged my duty when I lay the facts before you."

"Camel dung!"

The alien made a polite questioning noise.

"Your duty will be discharged when you have given my world back unharmed and returned life to every man who died in the Alliance fleet."

"I can see a concern for your planet but . . ." To Art even the

THEM commander's silences seemed amused. He wondered what the alien hoped to gain from this game. Jorf might lose ground over minor niceties of argument but the grizzled man had won the battle. He controlled the ship for the time being and if the instructions Art was hearing over the PA could be taken at face value, the entire THEM crew was surrendering with an orderly lack of violence as surprising as Japan's had been a generation ago. But, Art reflected, the Japanese had won the peace too. He turned back to the THEM staff officer.

"No doubt you're being totally co-operative," he began, "but I want to know how to run this ship. And please don't tell me it takes years. I've gone from diesels to FTL in something under ten months."

The staff officer's amusement was less obvious this time. "The ion drive is similar to your own," he began. "The FTL has an optical scanner locked into the holo. I don't know how it works but, basically, you take a sight on the star nearest your destination. The computer parallaxes the distance and you press the button."

"Does it always work?"

"I could give you a more accurate answer if every unreported ship would explain why. In any event, it works most of the time."

"What are all these consoles?"

"Weapons systems. Each covers one sector of the ship's perimeter. The commander co-ordinates from the secondary holo."

"Is the ship's captain the same as the fleet commander?"

"The fleet commander is with your captain."

"On my planet," Art observed acidly, "only women and politicians answer questions with a direct *non sequitur*."

"I am the flagship captain," the THEM said reluctantly.

Damned convenient coincidence, Art thought. *Out of a hundred captured staff officers I just happen to strike up a conversation with the right one.* "What's your name?"

"Jírhau." He pronounced it with a softened French "j."

"I don't wish to sound needlessly bloodthirsty," Art continued, "but I've had a trying day. I need accurate information far more than I need a full staff. Now tell me, Jírhau, are you *really* the captain of this ship?"

"You lead me down semantic by-ways replete with possibilities for misunderstanding—"

Art took a firm grip of his alpenstock.

"Yes, I am the captain." Even now Jírhau seemed amused.

"You overheard my commander and yours discussing a possible alliance," Art probed. "Since you've destroyed our planet, why shouldn't we keep you alive just long enough to return the compliment?"

"That is a decision which you must make."

Art frowned. What, he wondered, does one do next when a man facing a gun says, "Go ahead and shoot"?

Suddenly a lost thought returned. Art had seen enough technology in the last ten months to believe anything. "Are you human?" he asked. "Is that your true shape?"

This time Jírhau didn't try to conceal his laughter. "Every race has its legends of shape changers. What are they on your planet?"

"Werewolves," Art supplied. "But I was thinking of something a little closer to reality. Are you in control of the body standing before me or is somebody manning a robot console from a safe distance?"

"If you cut us, do we not bleed?"

Art had heard that somewhere else but he couldn't remember where. "Let me put it another way," he fumbled. "If I killed you, would you stay killed?"

"There are always transplants."

Art was tempted to swing his alpenstock but he didn't want to admit defeat.

Jorf's voice came tinny over the radio. "What's the real difference between you?" he was asking. "The Alliance set us up, you destroyed us. The Alliance is finished. At the moment the situation lacks symmetry."

"But is the Alliance finished?" the THEM commander was asking. Being several feet from Jorf's mike, his voice was even more faint. "You must remember this is a very minor battle. True, we have had some luck with the forces of your planet—extremely brave and able men, I might add. But if we were to face a first-class Alliance fleet instead of the worn-out junk they gave you, it's entirely possible you might have won."

Art wondered if all THEM were descended of used car salesmen.

"I have won," Jorf said.

"You've won this ship and its fleet. What about half a universe full of Alliance ships and planets?"

"You seem awfully anxious to have my insignificant little force on your side." From his toneless voice Art had little difficulty imagining the Arab's hooded gaze. The phrase had probably been more pungent before it came out of the translator.

Translator! Abruptly Art realized he wasn't overhearing suit radio at all. Somehow the ship's interpreter-computer had cut him into the conversation. He wondered if it was intentional. "You hear anything?" he asked McQuoyd.

The Belfast mate gave him a puzzled look and shook his head as he went back to trying to make some sense of THEM navigational instruments. Art turned back to the rigid captain in front of him. "Relax," he growled. "I'll give you a micro-second's warning if I decide to kill you."

"That will be sufficient," the alien said soberly, as his crossed palms dropped to his sides. Art tried not to be frightened.

This whole war was beginning to look like a con job. He wondered what the original squabble between THEM and the Alliance was about. Why had Earth been sucked into it? He wondered momentarily if men knee-deep in rice paddies had asked similar questions about America and the Soviet Union. But this time the man from the small planet was in a position to get some answers—if he could just learn how to ask the questions.

Art didn't know whether THEM were lying or just evading. Maybe it really was as the man before him had tried to say—a matter of semantics. Art had had troubles enough trying to interpret between different parts of Earth, each of which insisted on seeing tree$_1$ (palm) or tree$_2$ (fir) instead of some platonic idealization of a tree which an observer other than Art would probably only have labeled tree$_3$ (cottonwood). But if THEM were honestly trying to communicate, did he have to struggle with this vast secret amusement?

Possibly. Art remembered the way his hackles had risen when a Japanese aboard the *Nishrub* had explained, *"Yes [chuckle] my house burned down. Unimportant [vast smile and giggle]. My wife and both my sons were inside. No [hee-hee], no chance to save them."* It had taken Art some time to understand that for the Oriental this was politeness, a way of excusing the listener from condolences which should be saved for the funeral where wailing and hair pulling were proper.

Art wondered if these aliens had the slightest idea what he was talking about. Jorf seemed to understand them better. It was odd. The grizzled Arab had never been long on patience or reasoning. Now he seemed positively philosophical. Did that stink of camel dung and Moorish cooking have anything to do with it? Art sighed and steeled himself. "What caused the war between the Alliance and THEM?"

Jírhau shrugged. "If two people want something and there is only enough for one . . ." He left it dangling.

"What wasn't there enough of?"

Another smile. "Land, raw materials, all the things for which wars are fought."

"What specifically did you want from Earth?"

More smiles and shrugs. "The Alliance was arming this system. Is it not natural that we neutralize their influence?"

"Couldn't you have attempted a peaceful contact first?"

"*I* couldn't," Jírhau said pointedly.

"*Befohl ist Befohl,*" Eichmann had said. Every debacle from Calvary to Watergate had resulted from "just following orders." Art wished Jorf would stop his maundering with the fleet commander. Why not just kill all these snake-oil salesmen and take their chances learning how to run the ship?

He decided to try again. There had to be some way to crack through that secret mirth. "Do you know anything of Earth customs?"

"A little," Jírhau said.

"Do you marry, have children?"

"Of course."

"One wife at a time?"

"These things differ from planet to planet. Myself, I have one wife and one child. I am permitted another but it is not approved."

"So your world is overcrowded?"

"Whose isn't?"

"Did it never occur to you when embarking on this expedition that we poor planetbound primitives might take it into our heads to go destroy *your* planet, *your* wife, *your* child?"

"Life is a branching of possibilities," Jírhau said. "That one seemed rather remote."

"Does it still?"

Jírhau smiled. "I'm afraid it does. Nothing can elicit data which I do not possess. All charts and references to our home system auto-destructed at the moment of impact."

"What about the rest of the fleet?"

"There are standard operating procedures for surrender."

"I thought you never surrendered."

"Did you get that information firsthand from one of us?"

That, Art knew, was the hell of it. Every bit of knowledge about THEM had come from the Alliance. It was like trying to evaluate America from Russian descriptions. For the first time he wondered seriously if Earth had really joined the wrong side. Was there a right or wrong side? One of these days he would have to ask some Cambodian.

He shook himself out of this tail-swallowing logic. "You could have warned us. You could have told us to stay out of somebody else's war."

"Would you have listened?"

Art would have. Yet here he was in the Alliance fleet, just as this man was in THEM's. Behind that smile perhaps lay the same kind of bitterness.

And perhaps not. If only Art weren't so afraid. It had been fear, he knew, that sent the *Nishrub*'s men rampaging through this ship, killing everything that moved. Any thoughts of revenge for a destroyed Earth had been secondary. And if this alien didn't stop being amused Art knew fear was going to make him drive an alpenstock right through that smile. Maybe the stranger was telling the truth. But he was too damn smug about it.

The sons of bitches were all lying. Who ever heard of a crew that didn't know how to run a ship? He had to get Jorf away from that smooth-talking fleet commander long enough to warn him.

Bercovici and the mates were wandering about the bridge, study-ing flow charts and asking questions, punching consoles and raising eyebrows at some of the things that happened. Art wondered if either of the mates would understand his doubts. The trilingual engineer would be of no help. He hated all governments with a passion equally purple, living only for machinery and an occasional glass of Tyroler beer. The mates were able men but not particularly intelligent. Art often suspected Nessim was the smarter of the two but he lacked the Belfast man's blarney and always came out second in their eternal running argument.

Suddenly Art's ears popped and he felt air pressure drop. He was buttoning down his faceplate when Bercovici yelled, *"Pardone. Is hokay now."* The engineering officer hastily punched more keys on the console he was fiddling with. "Did I kill anybody?" he asked cheerfully.

A moment passed before a carefully neutral THEM voice said, "About four hundred enlisted personnel on their way to surrender."

"Surrender?" Bercovici asked in the same cheerful voice. "Oh, you mean that party with automatic weapons and gas grenades that was tearing along this way on the belt?"

There was no answer.

Art turned to Jírhau. "I thought you'd surrendered," he snarled.

Jírhau crossed hands before his chest. *"I* have."

Somewhere on the edge of his attention Jorf's voice was growing louder over the radio. "What's your big wheel's name?" Art asked.

"Jírllen." The alien pronounced the "ll" with that odd Welsh sound which English speakers mangle into Lloyd or Floyd without realizing they're the same.

"Is *jír* part of a name or a title?"

The alien was impressed. "You are observant," he smiled. "Actually it's a gender indicator. Other sexes begin their names with *jér, jár,* or *júr.*"

Art had a feeling he was learning more than he wanted to know about THEM customs. "How many potential enemies do I have aboard this ship?" he asked again.

Once more the amusement was back, tinged this time with a slight bitterness. "Your cheerful friend over there who depressurized part of the ship must know that more accurately than I."

Sonofabitch! Even Moonface was accomplishing something. Meanwhile Art stood here maundering and consistently getting the worst of it from this quick-witted *jír,* whatever that meant.

Suddenly Jorf's voice was so loud Art had to turn it down. "—we join forces and plunder the Alliance planets," the Arab was saying. "And then what?"

The THEM commander's answer was unintelligible. Art looked around the bridge. The *Nishrub*'s men were alert and keeping their distance from the bulk of the staff, who still stood with crossed palms.

Art unconsciously increased the distance between himself and Jírhau as Jorf and the alien commander came back to the bridge. The Arab shot Art a quick unfathomable glance, then turned briefly to Bercovici. *"Barakalúfik,"* he said, which is Moroccan for "blessed thanks."

He turned to the rest of the crew. Art poised to interpret, then realized the THEM machinery was doing it automatically.

"These, our conquered enemies, have offered us a magnificent opportunity." The Arab's usual gruff commentary rolled from the interpreter with studied elegance. "Meanwhile, a small dissident force has been crushed, thanks to the co-operation of all parties interested in keeping the peace.

"There will be difficult times ahead for all of us, but, with prudence and foresight, we shall win out. Great dangers also mean great opportunities."

Art listened unbelieving. Jorf would never spout any drivel that could even remotely be interpreted this way. He closed his faceplate to shut out the interpreter, trying to hear the grizzled Arab's original words. It was no use. The machine had taken over and was drowning out everything.

Art wondered if Jorf knew what was happening. He seemed oblivious as he gushed this happy nonsense. Then Art was really frightened. Maybe Jorf had finally flipped, fallen under the spell of this super snake-oil salesman who lost battles and won surrenders.

Jorf was looking straight at him. Art stared back, willing communication with those hooded eyes. "—to ensure security," the Arab was continuing, "all *Nishrub* personnel will recharge tanks immediately. Those THEM who have surrendered will be temporarily enclosed in the *Nishrub*'s hold while this larger ship is bled of air.

"Then we shall go through it compartment by compartment, sealing off emergency air outlets. When we have checked every space suit and rescue mask against inventories the ship will be pressurized again."

Nishrub men began cutting surprised THEM into small parties and herding them down the beltway. Jorf caught Art's eye and suddenly grinned. "Ahtt," he said, "I think THEM smarter than us."

"I know they are," Art mournfully agreed.

"Yah," Jorf said thoughtfully. "Maybe three days no food. Then we see how goddam smart."

CHAPTER NINE

Even though the routes were clearly marked on the loofah-shaped tracery, Art managed to lose himself and the dozen prisoners he was escorting. Finally a THEM pointed out the right direction. They climbed the last hundred meters through wreckage toward the spot where McQuoyd was overseeing the mass of THEM filing into the *Nishrub*'s one intact tank. To Art it seemed more as if THEM were doing it themselves while the Belfast mate blustered ineffectually. "How many so far?" Art asked.

"About twenty-one hundred."

"Twenty-three hundred fifty-one," a THEM corrected.

"How do you know?" Art asked. "You just got here."

The THEM gave him an odd look. "Don't you keep in touch with one another?"

"And you all have built-in radio or some such?"

"Naturally." The THEM filed into the tank. Art wondered who was in control here. THEM had been stripped of their weapons. To make sure they carried nothing else THEM had also been stripped of their clothes. Remembering Jorf's search for hidden breathing apparatus, Art wondered if a peep into an ear canal would reveal a miniaturized radio.

To hell with it, he decided. If it meant anything, THEM would not have revealed its existence so casually. He turned his prisoners over to McQuoyd. By the time he got back to the bridge somebody had realized it would be easier to instruct THEM still at large to go directly to where the *Nishrub* lay like a spent bullet.

Art found a sleeping compartment next to the bridge and reported his discovery to Jorf. They spent a few minutes dividing the *Nishrub*'s people into watches. Art was so exhausted he drifted off still in his suit.

Nessim shook him awake several hours later.

"What's new?" Art asked.

"All man is—" The mate gave an angry shrug and decided to forget his aversion to speaking Arabic with the ship's Talker. "We've broadcast the alarm for several hours," he said. "Flushed out a couple of hundred here and there. McQuoyd and Berkóvich are checking breathing gear inventories. Your tanks charged?"

Art checked and nodded.

"Good. Soon now we'll evacuate the ship."

"We're leaving?" Art was still sleepy and it took him a moment to realize the thin dark man meant they would let the air out, rather than take all the people off. "I hope everybody's been warned," he said.

"Why do you think I'm wasting time here with you?" the mate snapped.

"Oh! I thought you'd all be using that fancy interpreting machine now."

Nessim gave him an odd look. "You may not be as eloquent as that accursed computer," he finally said, "but at least we know which side you're on."

"*Ahtt!*" The unmistakable voice came through his suit radio.

"I'm here with Nessim," Art answered.

"Call muster."

Hours passed before Art thought he knew who was alive, who dead, who busy, asleep, or not understanding instructions, or what the hell? There seemed to be a hundred and seventy left of the *Nishrub*'s original two hundred. Finally they were all in the bridge, save for the half dozen who guarded the *Nishrub*. He rang the linguistic changes until everyone checked somebody else's air supply. Art checked Moonface's and was mildly surprised to find everything in order. "I guess we're ready," he finally sighed.

Bercovici punched a console and Art felt the slight bulge and stretch as his suit expanded in lowered pressure. He remembered how air had rushed endlessly through the *Nishrub*'s rent. How long would it take to empty this planet-sized ship of air?

It took less than a minute now that Bercovici knew what he was doing and had opened all the vents. "How long to pressurize again?" Art asked.

"Quite a while," the engineering officer explained. "There isn't much reserve aboard."

"You mean we're going to live in suits indefinitely?"

The trilingual engineer shook his head. "They electrolyze oxygen out of water," he explained, "but the rest of it isn't nitrogen. Probably they've dreamed up some special mix that won't tear a body apart so badly if they have a sudden pressure drop."

"It didn't seem to help the ones we killed."

"*Ahtt!*"

Art turned down his radio and waited for his ears to stop ringing.

Jorf had activated one of the loofah sponge maps. "Berkóvich will stay here," the Arab said. "One man guard his back." He pointed as Art interpreted. "The rest of us will go astern. From there we fan out and work our way toward the bow. Go slow. Take maybe days to get there but we make damn sure no THEM runs around loose. You see, you kill. Keep in touch. Use radio." Most of the party were on the beltway before Art finished running through his languages. It had, for Jorf, been an unusually long speech.

The stern was rounded and double-bottomed like the *Nishrub*'s but so immeasurably greater that Art was not conscious of any curvature. They assembled in what seemed to be a tool crib, though Art had only the vaguest notion what the tools were for. Jorf scuffled his foot and elicited another map, this one with its pulsating you-are-here spot at one end of the loofah tracery. He studied the multicolored arteries and began assigning a man to each. There were more passages than men. "We go this far," he said, "then come back down—"

There was no air at all in the ship now, apart from that inside the *Nishrub*'s one intact tank and each man's suit bottles. Art wondered if THEM were overhearing their radio. It was their ship. Art suspected THEM would have little difficulty avoiding this tiny search party if they put their minds to it. But Jorf's instructions were mostly "you go this way." Unless a THEM was actually watching him point at the loofah map . . .

"What if we run out of air?" the blue-eyed man asked in his bad French.

"Tell Berkóvich. He will feed air to your nearest outlet long enough

to recharge." Jorf looked levelly at his people. "But I don't want nobody run out of air before we come together again."

They began spreading out. Art promptly panicked. For a moment
he couldn't even remember which vein in the loofah tracery had been
assigned to him. When he did finally dredge this information from
his unwilling memory he wondered how he could ever patrol those
endless kilometers of passage alone. But with Jorf looking at him he
realized he was even more afraid of failure.

His passageway was barely wide enough for two men to pass. He
had known from its color on the loofah that there would be no beltway. What he didn't know was how to walk these endless kilometers
alone, flinching from each opening, wondering what waited around
each bend.

It had all been too easy. THEM shouldn't have given up without
a struggle. With his kind of luck Art knew he was going to find their
real stronghold—maybe even the real THEM. The ones he had killed
so far had been distressingly human. Art couldn't get away from the
suspicion that somewhere there lurked a controlling *something*—
probably with tentacles or mind control or even hairier possibilities.

The compartments he peered into were all empty. He was far from
living quarters. Possibly this part of the ship wasn't even normally
pressurized. He saw outlets for recharging air bottles but that could
mean anything. He tried one and after a first faint puff nothing
came out. In the vacuum he could hear nothing apart from the grunts
and mutterings that came over suit radio. Apparently nobody was
finding anything exciting.

The next compartment had supplies in orderly piles. The cartons
were ordinary corrugated cardboard. Art forgot to be frightened for
a moment. If these weren't loot from Earth—and surely there hadn't
been time for that! Then he realized any planet where humans lived
must also be inhabited by trees or some fibrous plant from which
paper could be made. Come to think of it, paper would probably turn
out to be the chief product of any advanced society. He tore at a
carton and it refused to open. Finally he found the tab and it split.
Inside were smaller cartons, each with the same stylized pictogram:
yucca, pineapple, artichoke? He wondered if it were edible. It
would be nice to try something different from those ghastly gruels
the *Nishrub* synthesized.

Synthesized . . . No wonder there were no really big storerooms aboard this planet-sized ship. Perhaps this was some delicacy beyond the capacities of a synthesizer. He shook a carton with sudden suspicion but it did not gurgle. When he tore it open grayish powder spilled out. Food? Drink? Narcotic? Medicine? For all he knew it might be glue.

The next compartment was half full of a different sized cardboard box, with a pictogram of some improbable animal with a single horn and wings. When Art opened one the same grayish powder spilled out. To hell with it. He still couldn't hear anything in the vacuum but now he could feel vibration.

He went back out into the narrow corridor and his fear returned. He took a deep breath and tried to screw up his courage again. He left the cubbyholed storage area and came nearer the rhythmic throbbing. He put his faceplate to the bulkhead which stretched endlessly to one side of the corridor. The slosh-gurgle became louder. He continued cautiously to the next crossover and scuffled a loofah map into life. If he was reading it right, this must be a recycling tank. He was ashamed of his funk now. There were grunts and wheezes, an occasional obscenity as somebody stumbled under the unfamiliar burden of a suit in full gravity. Art checked his machine pistol. It was loaded, safety off.

He came to another gasketed hatch. It was barely large enough for a man encumbered with space suit and air tanks. The hatch was dogged down as securely as all the others Art had encountered since he first heard the rhythmic slosh of pumping machinery. But this hatchway was wet around the edges. A puddle on the deck was rapidly turning into brown crud as water boiled away in the vacuum. The tank had to be a recycling fermenter. What puzzled Art was the wet footprints that led from the puddle, down the companionway in front of him.

It had to be one of the *Nishrub*'s men. The puddle was where a man had stood dogging the hatch shut again. The first dozen steps were clotted slime but from there on he recognized the cleated footprint of a space suit. Relaxing slightly, he followed the drying tracks. Soon there was only an occasional gob where fermenting waste had dropped from the suit.

He wondered what the crewman had been doing inside the tank.

Then he remembered the *Nishrub*'s people had all been inside a tank when they hit. Why, Art wondered, couldn't he think of obvious things like that? He wondered how many hiding places he had left unsearched behind him. Then he compared the footprint with the sole of his own suit. He laughed. It was a *Nishrub* man.

He followed the trail of fetid slime, thankful that in a space suit he didn't have to smell it. Finally the throb-surge of the pump lessened and they left the tank behind. He still hadn't caught up with the other man. Whoever he was, he was lost. This was Art's passage. Which meant the other man's was going unsearched. Another crossing appeared. Art approached it cautiously and saw the smeared bulkhead where the man in the filth-clotted suit had turned a corner. Art followed.

Finally he traced the man through another door into what turned out to be a bathroom. The man was showering the crud off his suit, having the devil's own time with water which evaporated in the vacuum and created tremendous clouds of mist instead of jetting where he wanted it to go. "Did you find anything in there?" Art asked.

The space-suited figure emerged from the shower. He was carrying a machine pistol just like Art's. It was pointing straight at Art's stomach. The safety was off.

Art felt himself melt into a puddle of panic, restrained from flowing all over the deck only by the space suit which contained his paralyzed body. "No!" he croaked. "It's me, Art the Talker!"

The man in the newly cleaned space suit gestured. Expecting a *mitrailleusade* any instant, Art turned gingerly around. He felt the other man fiddling with connections on the back of his suit. *Going to cut off my air!*

There was a suddenly different sound to Art's radio and he could no longer hear the grunts and sighs of the rest of the crew. "There," a strange voice said in English. "We're on another wave length. Perhaps we can talk."

"What do you want?" Art babbled.

There was a nervous chuckle. "Nothing like mutual interests," the other voice said.

"Mutual interests in what?" Art chattered.

"In staying alive while the rest of these cretinous assassins accumulate scars and raw material for sagas."

Very cautiously, Art began turning. "Who are you?" The cocked weapon was still aimed at him. "Please!" Art said.

"After you," the stranger replied.

Abruptly, Art realized he still held his own weapon. He weighed the chances of aiming and firing before the other could pull the trigger. Not even Jorf, he suspected, would buck those odds. Moving very slowly, he lowered the automatic by its strap. The stranger gestured and Art preceded him into another compartment. It was a lounge. The chairs were as odd-shaped as elsewhere aboard this ship but Art fell into one an instant before his legs dissolved.

In the silence no longer punctuated with breathing and grunting he could hear two-toned THEM radio faintly in the background. He didn't know why it startled him that the stranger had switched over to a THEM frequency. He couldn't very well be anything else. But . . . Art was encouraged by the fact that he was still breathing. "What do you want?" he asked.

"I want to surrender."

Art stared. "We've been broadcasting instructions for hours. Why didn't you turn yourself in?"

There was a moment of silence. Finally the other said, "Your people display a regrettable propensity for overreaction."

"Overreaction? You mean we get bent out of shape just because you attack us?"

"Are you native to this system?"

"I didn't volunteer to go chasing off somewhere else looking for a fight," Art snapped.

"Oh come now. You're all volunteers. But you may be my kind of volunteer—in the passive rather than the active voice of said verb."

"You got 'volunteered' too?" Art asked.

The THEM put down his weapon. "Something like that," he said.

Art looked at the gun. Chances were the other man could still reach it first. "So you want to surrender . . ."

"I also wish proper treatment."

Art wondered if Jorf's remark about dieting THEM into a more co-operative attitude had carried over the radio. "Have you been listening to us?" he asked.

"Naturally. Don't you monitor our communications?"

"It doesn't do much good unless you know the language."

"The Alliance is always careful that way," the THEM agreed.

"Speaking of language, I thought Bercovici turned off that interpreter."

"If you mean that ham-fisted cretin who fouled up every servo system aboard this flagship, you are correct."

"Then how are we communicating?"

"I happen to be one person who took sufficient interest to waste a fortnight learning one of your planet's languages."

"You're actually speaking English?"

"Does it sound like Baluchistani?"

Art gauged the distance between himself and the guns.

"Oh, crapulent coprophagous Christ!" the THEM sighed. With the toe of his freshly showered suit he kicked the gun toward Art. "Go ahead and shoot. You need me worse than I need you."

"I have orders to kill every THEM who hasn't turned himself in," Art said.

"When you write your memoirs remember to say you were just following orders."

"In return for not killing you—" Art began.

"You preserve the memory that I did likewise. Also, I'll be less coy about answering questions."

"Why?"

The THEM laughed. "I've always thought this was an immoral war. More precisely, providing *I* survive, I give not a soaring adlunar coition who wins."

"Perhaps we do have mutual interests. What really happened anyway? Did Earth get sucked into somebody else's civil war?"

"Did you ever wonder why the Alliance training officers spoke only Earth languages?"

Art hadn't. "You trying to tell me they're Earthmen with dyed hair?"

CHAPTER TEN

The THEM shook his head. "They're not from Earth. Can't we get out of these suits and talk normally?"

"What's wrong with this?"

"It's radio. Either your people listen in or mine do."

"Can't you find an unused wave length?"

"We're on one now but sooner or later another ship out there's going to monitor us."

Art had momentarily forgotten the THEM fleet surrounding the disabled flagship. He thought a moment. "Can you make this compartment air-tight?"

"I can make any compartment air-tight. I only spent three days swimming in shit because I believe in sane precautions when the insane command."

"Switch me back to my own wave length." *Jorf isn't going to like this,* Art thought. But it would be worth it if he could just get solid information. He turned his back and the THEM fiddled with something again. The grunts and wheezes of the *Nishrub*'s men came back. "Bercovici," Art called. *"Sono io, il parlatore. Ho bisogno d'ossigeno."*

"Where are you? What happened?"

"I must've sprung a leak." Art tried to describe his location. The THEM opened an emergency outlet and air began flowing into the compartment. Cautiously, he cracked his faceplate. He smiled.

"Okay," Art called. "That's enough."

"Ciao," Bercovici said. Art turned off his radio and opened his own faceplate.

Now that Art could see him more clearly, the THEM seemed quite old. His violet hair had changed to a rusty brown, which Art supposed must be the equivalent of graying. His face displayed a cynical wisdom not untinged with the amusement on every THEM's face. But perhaps this old man was willing to share the joke.

"So why don't the Alliance officers speak their own language?" Art asked. He remembered now that some people had wondered about this in the early stages of preparing for the THEM invasion. The explanation, he remembered, had been that since the Alliance men had been specially trained to serve on Earth and already knew the languages there would be time for philologists and cultural exchangeniks once the war was over—providing Earth and the Alliance won.

"It might have been difficult to explain why we and the Alliance speak the same language," the THEM said.

"So it *is* a civil war!"

"Not exactly."

Art glanced at the machine pistol.

"Oh, festering feces!" the THEM snapped. "If you want simple answers you'll get what you deserve."

Art wondered if he sounded this way to Moonface and the other eight balls aboard the *Nishrub*.

"I don't wish to belabor the obvious," the THEM continued. "But humanoids evolve on planets best suited for them. Since humanoids consist of the usual sexes with the usual appetites, history, no matter what their planet of origin, displays a certain tired sameness."

"I've always known humans like to kill one another," Art said.

"Have you studied the art of war?"

"Not willingly."

"History is all we have," the THEM said. "Are you familiar with, say, the Tlaxcalan Republic?"

Art thought Tlaxcala was in Mexico. He had never known it was a republic.

"In the Roman sense," the THEM said, "which coincides with a later meaning except *cosa nostra* is 'our thing' and *res publica* is Latin for 'public thing.' In a republic the vote belongs to those who own property and can raise troops."

"What are you getting at?" Art asked.

"On the way to Mexico Cortez fought a week-long battle with the Tlaxcalans, who concluded his gods were stronger and promptly switched sides. Can you guess why they so willingly helped a foreign invader with two hundred men conquer fifteen million Aztecs?"

"I suppose the pickings looked better."

"Only partly correct. Does their being totally surrounded by Aztec territory suggest anything?"

"They were besieged?"

"Their borders remained stable despite constant fighting."

Art frowned and wondered what the THEM was getting at. "By the way," he asked, "do you have a name?"

"Jeroboam."

"I can probably reach that gun faster than you," Art growled.

"All right already. Honorifics bore me. My name's Baz. Go back far enough and it means 'noble predator' or some such self-contradictory nonsense. I'm old and have published enough academic flapdoodle to be called Járbaz. I'm vain enough to prefer Jírbaz."

Art suspected he had just received a lightning indoctrination but Baz-whatever was still fighting another war. "The Aztecs lived by terror and extortion, not even bothering to occupy conquered territories. Just came around periodically to raid for food and victims. They could have taken Tlaxcala any time but it was a handy little place, not too far out of town."

"Weekend wars?"

"Or hunting parties. It gave young men of noble family something to do. Parenthetically, Aztecs and Tlaxcalans spoke the same language."

"I get the feeling you're trying to tell me something," Art said. "But no matter how you slice it, I see no excuse for not killing you. I'm not bloodthirsty; just a professional coward who could never sleep nights if I thought you were alive for a second chance."

"There are always second chances unless you get all of us out there."

"A nice massacre might convince them of our sincerity."

"Just as you convinced the North Vietnamese?"

Art gave up. "What are you after?" he finally asked. "Do you want us to join you against the Alliance?"

"Was there a Tlaxcalan Republic in your United Nations when we arrived?"

"I see," Art said. "We didn't even fight the Alliance when they came."

"Neither did the coastal tribes around Veracruz when Cortez arrived. Do you remember their names?"

"So no matter what we do, a superior culture is going to destroy or absorb us?"

"Are the Japanese extinct?"

"Have you ever heard of Dogpatch Logic?" Art asked. "It entails the extortion of a straight answer by application of grievous bodily harm."

"So shoot. I'm irreplaceable. Has a THEM ever volunteered information before?"

"How the hell would I know?" Art grumped.

"You won't unless you listen. Perhaps you think I savor the bliss of forcing two liters into a one-liter brain?"

"What were you on this ship?" Art asked. "Court jester?"

"Official historian. For which you may read, 'librarian.'"

"There's only so much air in this compartment," Art said. "And if my captain decides I'm lost he may regard me as indispensable and mount a search party."

Baz cracked a valve on his suit tanks and let more air into the room. "There goes my reserve, in case you suspect ulterior motives. Do you know the derivation of 'education'?"

"Comes from a couple of Latin roots meaning 'lead out.'"

"Precisely. I can lecture for aeons and you'll remain unconvinced unless I can draw on familiar examples and make you see the knowledge already in your own cerebrum."

"So where are we?" Art sighed.

"We were discussing longevity."

Art wondered how he could keep getting sidetracked from a subject which had always been near and dear. How would Jorf handle this kind of situation? Jorf was uneducated, unsophisticated, but he knew how to separate the meat from the gravy. "Are you a disgruntled nationalist from some gobbled-up planet?" Art asked.

"Not exactly. More like a member of a minor political party."

"*Ahtt!*" Though his suit radio was as low as it could be without turning it off Jorf's shout startled him. "Yessir!" Art replied.

"Where the hell you? Why you don't answer?"

"Been having trouble with my suit," Art lied. "Everything's okay now though."

"Berkóvich says pressurized compartment somewhere near you. Something jammed and he can't release it. You be careful."

"I will," Art promised. He wondered why he was lying, then abruptly knew. Jorf would kill this THEM or toss him in the *Nishrub*'s tank with the others. Somehow Art had to get some real information.

"You hear that?" he asked.

Baz nodded. "Is that the affirmative gesture in your culture?"

Art reassured him. "But sooner or later we face my commander, who is long on action and can be very short on explanations. If you're as interested in your survival as I in mine, perhaps you'd better accelerate this education."

"I wish I could."

"How many THEM are there?"

"The number would be meaningless. Something over a thousand inhabited planets, I would guess."

"How many ships?"

"Perhaps three per planet."

"Does the Alliance have more or less?"

Baz gave him an odd look. "We're pretty evenly matched," he finally said.

"Does your side also recruit planet-bound primitives like us?"

"Whenever they're sufficiently advanced to be assimilated into our society."

"How advanced is Earth?"

"You won." Baz shrugged and added, "From a historical viewpoint, you're behind in some things, rather ahead of us in others."

"Exactly what the Alliance ambassador said."

"The most successful technique for lying is to tell the truth on all unimportant points."

"Your fleet commander seems in his labyrinthine way to be suggesting we join him against the Alliance. Would we gain anything by such a switch?"

"No. Nor would you lose."

"Then why shouldn't we just kill you all?"

"I thought we'd covered that already."

"*Ahtt!*"

"Yessir."

"Who the hell you talking to?"

Oooooooooooohhhhhhh shit! Why didn't I remember to turn down that radio? He wondered if it was a Freudian slip. Any more evasions would place him in an impossible position—and probably the THEM too. "I've captured a THEM," he said, and switched abruptly to Arabic. "Or rather, he captured me, then surrendered. This one sees the wisdom of co-operating on a full stomach."

"Bring him to end of passage."

"What does he want?" Baz asked.

It was Art's turn to be puzzled. "I thought you understood Earth languages."

"Only English. Once you turned off the interpreter—"

"Then the captives in the hold can't listen in on us any more?"

Baz grinned. "One of the few correct moves that ham-fisted mechanic playing with our consoles has made."

Art guessed he had learned something useful—if it were true. He gestured and began closing his faceplate. Then he remembered Baz had no air. "Got to recharge some tanks if we're going to keep this one alive," he said.

"Hokay," came Bercovici's cheerful voice.

Moments later the THEM's bottles were refilled and they went down the corridor. Art walked behind with the machine pistols. He worried about Jorf. The Arab might take it in his head to shoot this THEM on sight. And Art had disobeyed instructions too. But the captain only asked, "You learn something?"

"I think so," Art said. The gravity flickered momentarily and he struggled against nausea.

Jorf turned to the THEM. "Any more of you running around loose?"

Baz looked at Art. "I doubt it," he said when Art had translated. "But I don't really know."

Art tried to fill Jorf in on what he had learned.

"All right," Jorf finally said. "Take him where you and Bercovici's bodyguard can keep your eyes on him. Tonight you give me a full report."

"Did you understand any of that?" Art asked as they rode a belt-way back to the bridge.

"No, but since I'm still alive, I presume you're to interrogate me."

"You keep talking about survival," Art said, "but so far you've offered no suggestions. If you were from my planet, what would you do?"

"Something probably far different from what you'll do since I can no more think like you than you like me. I would imagine though, that primitive man knows more about survival than the average civilized sophisticate."

"Primitive man usually kills any stranger imprudent enough to ignore the first warning spear."

"Exactly."

"But you knew I wouldn't do it." Art sighed.

"Your commander would. But you and I are from a different mold. This way," the THEM parenthesized. Art followed him down a branching in the beltway and a moment later they were on the bridge.

"Allo," Bercovici said. "I got that compartment to drop pressure again."

"I left the door open," Art explained. "Here's a present for you."

The engineering officer studied Baz. "How do you communicate with the rest of the fleet?" he asked.

"He only speaks English," Art explained.

"*Dreck!*" Bercovici said. "*Merd! HOOvno!*"

"Is there any way we can use that interpreter without cutting in the whole damn fleet plus every prisoner in the tank?"

"I'm afraid not," Baz said.

Art sighed and began interpreting. He could rephrase one language into another with no more conscious effort than a typist. Then suddenly he found himself actually listening.

"It's a simple tonal language, one high, one low tone. The two pitches you hear on the radio represent the rhythm of phrases *en clair*—not really a code at all. Each sentence is paraphrased several times to eliminate any ambiguity. The only reason for using it is clarity over distances."

"Drums!" Art exclaimed.

Bercovici and Baz stared.

"African drum language. No wonder it sounded familiar!"

"Can anyone understand it?" Bercovici asked.

"Anyone who understands the language," Baz said.

"You learned English in a couple of weeks," Art said. "How long would it take you to teach me your language?"

"A couple of years."

"That hard?" Art didn't believe it. He had learned languages in less than a month.

"Actually," Baz explained, "it's a very easy language. But you asked how long it would take *me* to teach it. The *machine* could probably give you a working knowledge in two or three days."

"Starting when?"

"Whenever you're ready to go to sleep." Baz turned to Bercovici. "Not that way!" he snapped. "You've got to feed the co-ordinates in first." He punched something into the keyboard.

"Aaaaaaaaahhhhhh!" Bercovici said.

"I thought you were a librarian," Art growled. "How come you're also an engineer?"

"Esophageal excrement!" Baz sighed. "You're an interpreter. Therefore you cannot drive a car or use a typewriter?"

Art wondered if he would ever win an exchange with THEM. "This tonal language," he began, "is it the only language THEM speak?"

"Of course not. Every planet has local tongues. But if you want to trade or communicate you learn Basic."

"Perhaps everyone ought to learn it," Art mused. "It'd make my job easier." Nonexistent was what he meant.

"There are numerous precedents on your own planet," Baz supplied. "When the Japanese started building a navy they discovered their own tongue so bereft of nautical terminology that logs were kept in English right up until the time when the disadvantages became obvious."

"Meanwhile," Art mused, "we must learn to survive. Who is our worst enemy—you, the Alliance, or ourselves?"

Baz gave him a sad smile. "You still don't understand, do you? Now that it's finally happened people back home will remember my warnings. Since I was right I shall be roundly hated. Ah well . . . I can't say I'm glad it happened. But I'm amused. Despite the improbability of such an event, the laws of Entropy and Murphy occasionally concatenate into some approximation of poetic justice."

"Please," Art groaned. "I've got to tell my captain something."

"Of course you do. Tell him the rabbit shot the hunter."

"What the hell are you getting at?"

"The Alliance—THEM—can't you understand? There are no sides. We're all the same people."

CHAPTER ELEVEN

It took Art a moment to digest it. Then all the little bits dropped into place. This was why the THEM had tried to prepare him with stories about the Tlaxcalan hunting preserve. He supposed the alien wanted to show him that cruelty was no novelty in Earth's history.

Tasmania had been opened to colonization by setting out poisoned baits until there were no natives left. The man who gave Amherst College his name had solved an Indian problem by distributing smallpox-infected blankets. Hitler had . . . "Okay," Art said. "So what else is new? Do you take turns?"

"The Alliance sets up the target, arms the natives so it won't be too easy. THEM delivers the punch."

"*Punch!*" Art exclaimed. "I knew it!"

Baz looked a question at him.

"Do you know what science fiction is?"

The alien was thoughtful. "In a primitive culture I suppose it would be wildly inaccurate. Are you periodically devastated by creatures with impossible metabolisms and no possible use for an Earth-type planet?"

Art winced. "I used to read a lot of it. Since the Alliance ambassador showed up I've been remembering old plots trying to guess what was really up. *Punch* is a story by Fred Pohl. If somebody'd remembered it in time Earth might still be alive."

"What makes you believe Earth is dead?"

Abruptly Art realized he had been taking something else for granted.

"Maybe Earth lives," Bercovici said, when Art had translated. "I won't know until I figure out this radio."

Art thought a moment. It would be nice to have a few thousand Earth troops up here. But unless there were some ships he didn't know about they'd have to flap their arms pretty hard.

"You'd better win," Baz said, "for I'm about to burn my last bridge." He shouldered Bercovici aside and began punching information into the console.

"Does this one handle radio too?" Art asked.

"You can do anything from any one of these consoles."

"Providing you know how," Bercovici added. "Unfortunately, I was never an expert—even for Earth radio."

Baz stepped back. "You're on an Alliance channel now and hooked into an Earth-oriented antenna."

Art cleared his throat, then hesitated. "Jorf," he called over suit radio, "should I try to call Earth?"

"No!" The grizzled Arab's voice came tinny over the radio. "You listen. You find something you call me."

"Yessir," Art said.

Behind the ice asteroid and with power off the *Nishrub* had been unable to hear anything. Art didn't really expect to hear anything now, but to his surprise the air was full. The problem with THEM radio was not reception. It was selection. THEM's amplifiers were picking up everything from ground-plane submarine communications to line-of-sight drivel from tenth-of-a-watt walkie-talkie toys. Everything from Radio Luxembourg to the kid in the park's model airplane control was pouring from the bridge speakers in ceaseless cacophony.

"Can't you fine tune it?" Art asked. The gravity flickered and he steadied himself with a hand on the console. Baz diddled controls and a moment later Art recognized a familiar voice.

"—since destruction of the Allied fleet, resignation, business as usual seem the order of the day. Yet in the back of every man's mind lies that unanswerable question: What next?

"There have been token bombings. An impartial observer might point out that in normal times we kill more each day in our own wars, banditries, and auto accidents. Yet that apocalyptic voice assures us we are under attack. One can only conclude that there is more to come. Undoubtedly it will be worse.

"And now to Roger Mudd in Washington."

"Good evening, Walter. The attitude is grave here. Pentagon-Alliance sources admit destruction of the Allied fleet. So far as we know, no THEM ship was damaged. Tracking stations report the bulk of THEM is orbiting between Mars and Jupiter in the asteroid belt. Until now only a few advance scouts have penetrated cislunar space to bomb Earth. The Alliance training station and Moon Base do not answer signals and must be presumed destroyed. When asked if he was considering surrender the supreme commander's only comment was 'no comment.' "

Bercovici fingered the tip of his alpenstock as he studied the captive THEM.

"Observers are puzzled by THEM's failure to follow through after their initial strike against Earth. Opinion is sharply divided between those who presume the whole planet's 'open city' declaration will be respected by an enemy reputed to respect no rules, and between those optimists who believe the Alliance fleet in the micro-second before its destruction managed to inflict serious losses upon THEM. But in the absence of reports from the battle zone, all is conjecture. If Earth has won a victory, it is perhaps the best-kept secret in this security-conscious capital."

Art turned to Baz. "What happened? Why didn't you destroy Earth?"

Baz gave a nervous smile. "Any answer would be equally self-serving and unbelievable."

"Try one," Art said.

"You might say we don't bomb defenseless civilians. But considering the way we annihilated your fleet, that reasoning may seem specious. You will probably assume though, that it's because we surrendered before there was time."

Bercovici seemed to be controlling himself with difficulty but Art was becoming used to the involuted ways of THEM. "No doubt there's an explanation somewhere behind that contradiction," he said. "But it might take hours of frustration to find it. I have it on your own authority that you disapprove of THEM-Alliance foreign policy. But for it to exist, somebody must approve. What are *their* justifications?"

Baz shrugged. "It keeps troublemakers off the streets."

Art wondered if this was the kind of blinding light Saul saw on the road to Damascus. Suddenly the whole thing was beautifully clear. And not without precedents on Earth.

He remembered carpers who explained away the Spanish conquest

of America as a convenient way to handle a veteran problem when
the last Moor in Spain surrendered in that conveniently memorable
year of 1492. "So you take all your wild-eyed young fire-breathers
and turn them loose on somebody else instead of letting them mug
the solid citizens at home?"

Baz nodded. "In addition, once all those primitives insane enough
to volunteer for a space war against an unknown enemy have been
eliminated it's not difficult to absorb the remainder of the population
into our economy."

The concept was so beautiful in its simplicity that Art forgot to
be outraged. "So that's why the Alliance insisted on volunteers only."

"Exactly," Baz said. "Societies run more smoothly when anyone
with a lust for violent death is permitted to acquire firsthand experience, preferably before he's shot his lust into the gene pool. Of course
one occasionally gets those who volunteered only to escape an in-
tolerable alternative."

Art gave him a sharp look.

"Welcome to the club," Baz grinned.

"Won't a few centuries of this kind of selective breeding turn you
into a pretty bovine lot?"

"We've explored half the known universe without discovering any
nonhuman life as intelligent as you deem your swine and porpoises."
Baz shrugged. "But then, primitives always have an exaggerated
opinion of nonhuman intelligence. Talking animal legends and all
that." He paused. "But now, you see, the system has been skewed
with a new variable . . ."

"Because Earth won?"

"Not Earth. There's only one Earthman who's really dangerous."

Later Art was to remember and wonder if this was the opening of
a campaign to induce him to kill the man who had saved his life—and
Earth's. But it was lost in the flood of new data as he tried to understand what the alien was, through him, teaching Bercovici.

The engineering officer must be something of a genius in his own
line to have worked out what he already knew of THEM controls.
Now with Baz's coaching the trilingual engineer was rapidly taking
over complete control of the ship. Watching bemused as the engineer's hands played over the console Art finally asked, "Can you tell
from that gadgetry if there're any more THEM hiding out?"

"There will never be a machine that some man cannot outwit," Baz said. "But you could check personnel records and find out how many were unaccounted for."

"I suppose so," Art said. "But how about the ones we killed?"

"Personnel records include a health profile from constant monitoring. Death shows up as extremely poor health."

Art decided this was sufficiently important to call Jorf. He turned up his suit radio, then realized there were easier ways. He boomed a guarded announcement in Arabic over THEM's PA system.

"How do I know he's telling the truth?" Jorf growled.

Baz began explaining in English. "Actually," he continued, "you might as well use the shipboard computer-interpreter. It's only a machine."

"How do I know you're telling the truth?" Jorf persisted.

"After the aid and comfort I've given, where will I be if you don't win?" Baz asked.

Jorf had been growing increasingly aware of how long it would take to search this planet-sized ship, and of the thousands of ways his tiny party could be outwitted or avoided. Abruptly, he called off the compartment-by-compartment search and spent the rest of the afternoon conferring with Art over which of the *Nishrub*'s people could best spend their time learning to man the THEM ship while the others pulled guard duty. There was another momentary flicker as the gravity shifted. "Can you do anything about that?" Art asked the alien.

"Afraid not," Baz said. "You damaged something pretty basic."

"What?"

"The whole engineering crew. You'd've gotten better value if you'd kept them and killed the lot you found here on the bridge."

"Is it going to fail completely?"

Baz shrugged. "Your engineer probably knows more about it than I."

There was sudden crushing weight and for an instant Art thought he was coming apart. It hadn't lasted more than a fraction of a second but that was enough for Art to know there was still another way he could die. Bercovici and the alien were pale. *"Giuseppe cornuto!"* the engineer muttered, and went back to playing with a console.

THEM technology, as near as Art could tell, was the same as the *Nishrub*'s, only this larger ship had more complex machinery. Running it, he supposed, would be largely a matter of wiping dust from the knobs and reading instructions. Art picked up a manual. The stylized arrows pointing up or down before each word had to be tone indicators.

Baz pointed to an unoccupied console and showed him how to make the machine read out loud. Within an hour Art had mastered orthography and pronunciation. He wondered how long it would take him to understand what he was saying.

It was an exceedingly regular language, he saw, undoubtedly a very old one. It was methodical as Chinese, which has long since worn away the rough edges of irregular verbs. Some day English would say *goed* instead of *went,* as *worked* had already supplanted *wrought.* But that was assuming anyone still spoke English a century from now. THEM would be easier to teach the *Nishrub*'s mixed bag of misfits. It was, Art suspected, the wave of the future. He wondered if Moonface would bloom under the aegis of literacy.

"What the hell you doing?" Jorf asked.

Art explained.

"What you mean, we all got to learn THEM talk? We win, didn't we?"

"You're not really an Arab," Art said.

Jorf understood instantly. "You right," he said, and Art was spared the ordeal of explaining the Moslem conquest and how a lanugage from one tiny corner of Arabia had spread over half the world, supplanting countless native tongues including the Latin and Berber once spoken in Morocco. History was replete with barbarians who had conquered older and more sophisticated peoples only to be absorbed into them.

But Art had been puzzled by something more immediate. "Don't you think we ought to call Earth?" he asked, "at least let them know we're alive?"

Jorf's hooded gaze rested briefly on him. The man really did look like a hawk. There was that peculiar flicker to his unwavering eyes —like a nictitating membrane—an appraisal as unnerving as an eagle's. Jorf was as far from the emotional Semite stereotype as Art could imagine. He wondered if the graying bullet-headed man ever felt any emotion. There were times when it seemed almost as if he felt some fatherly liking for Art. But Art could never be sure what this cheerful murderer was thinking.

"Later," Jorf said. "People on Earth aren't the only ones listen."

Art wondered if the THEM fleet surrounding them could send over their commanders as hostages.

"Not very practical," Baz said. "You've got problem enough with the captives from this ship. Besides, they'd probably try something cute like sending the wrong man."

Jorf gave him a sharp look. "Were you listening in when they tried that aboard this ship?"

"Of course. Though your method of discouraging subterfuge produced immediate results, its effect on that unfortunate messman in masquerade persuaded me to wait until the situation had stabilized before risking a similar welcome."

"Those ships out there," Jorf asked. "Will they stay surrendered?" He waited while Art interpreted.

"As long as it suits them," the THEM said.

Art wanted to ask when it might not suit them but Jorf had withdrawn into himself. "Your machine interprets every language?" he finally asked.

"Only those programmed into it."

"How about codes?"

"It's only a machine," Baz explained. "It can analyze and synthesize but that takes time unless someone helps it along with advance information—like a basic syntax."

While Art was struggling to render these concepts in Arabic, Jorf asked, "Why does THEM radio always use code? You can't transmit voice?"

"We transmit voice and pictures as well as Earth," Baz said primly. "But habit happens to coincide with convenience. Every child knows the tone code. Over distance and interference it's more intelligible than voice."

Art injected a short dissertation on the tonal nature of the THEM-Alliance language. He was explaining how some Earth languages had as many as seven tones when Jorf abruptly grunted "Flatnose!"

Art and Baz stared.

"Flatnose!" Jorf repeated. "Black people south of desert. Speak two-tones. Three hundred years my people sell them to America. *Now* they all Muzlim. You talk flatnose," he snorted. "No wonder we win."

There was an uncomfortable silence. Art wondered how much Baz knew of the slave trade on Earth or the ironic twist which made its victims renounce English for a Swahili argot created out of Arabic and Bantu to facilitate the traffic in their grandmothers.

Meanwhile Bercovici had finally locked into the right wave length. From the despair in the voice it was obvious that no answer was expected but duty impelled someone to go on repeating, "All units report. Any ship of the Earth-Alliance fleet please report to HQ."

Art looked at Jorf. The silence stretched. Finally the grizzled Arab said, "Okay. You talk."

Art glanced at Bercovici. When the engineer nodded he began speaking. He couldn't remember how many light-minutes they were from Earth but it wasn't until he had nearly finished his report of the *Nishrub*'s demise and their adventures aboard the THEM flagship that the droning 'all units report' stopped in midsentence with an excited "Hey, chief!"

It was several minutes after that before a reply came.

"Gollywog placidate crony blame presage sturdy unfit nether—"

"Oh Christ!" Art groaned.

Baz laughed. "Captain report personally earliest possible after securing prisoners and—"

"You may as well cut the secret agent crap," Art told the radio. "A captured THEM's breaking it and he's not even hooked into his computer."

Minutes passed and finally Art realized HQ was going to continue their ineffectual code games. "Transmit *en clair* any language," he finally snapped. "The only guy up here with time to play games is THEM. If you want us to use him for an interpreter, on thy head be it."

There was an interminable time lag, then came an angry stripe-laden voice. "Who is in command up there?"

The time lag between transmissions had palled long ago. Jorf was busy picking Bercovici's brains. The mates drifted in and out, not arguing for once. The cook had finally coaxed a meal out of the synthesizer. One item in particular fascinated Art. It looked like an artichoke—but without the choke, and seemed to furnish its own butter. "Did you synthesize this?" he asked.

The cook was a short spare man from Djogjakarta with a pronounced tendency toward curry. "No way," he grinned, and produced a carton. It was from the storeroom Art had discovered and ignored, with the picture outside and the gray powder inside.

"Do you grow them?"

The cook shrugged. "Just add water."

"And you get that?" The vegetable was perfect, without the slightest flaw in vein or fiber. "I don't believe it," Art said.

Baz pulled a leaf from his and chewed. "Molecular memory," he said, as if that explained everything.

Art looked at him.

"You already have the beginnings," the alien explained. "This is merely the next step beyond permanent press."

"Captain or commander in charge report immediately!" a voice boomed in English.

"Tell him I'm eating," Jorf grunted.

Art did, suddenly pondering what the grizzled skipper had on his mind. If Earth was still unharmed maybe they could . . . But he had been with Jorf long enough to know there would be no easy way.

"Everybody eat?" Jorf asked.

"Yes sair!" the cook enthused.

"Oops!" Bercovici said, and broke into a smart trot.

Ten minutes later every man who had eaten had the trots.

"THEM's Revenge?" Art asked. "Or are you trying to poison us?" In the Mediterranean he had been afflicted every time he crossed from Spain to Africa. Chances were they'd soon get used to the different intestinal flora aboard this ship. Jorf was looking speculatively at the THEM. He growled something unintelligible as the *Nishrub*'s people straggled pale and wan back to the bridge. "Okay," he yelled, "we get ready now."

"For what?" Art asked.

Jorf pointed at the holo. The tiny red flecks of THEM were beginning to move.

CHAPTER TWELVE

Art began shouting the off watch awake.

"You don't expect your people to man consoles?" Baz exclaimed.

"What else?" Jorf asked.

Baz shrugged. "You've got a whole staff of trained men down there in a tank. They're just as interested in living as you."

"Will they fight?"

"What choice have they?"

Jorf's decision was instantaneous. "Bring prisoners back to bridge," he yelled. "THEM man consoles; we man THEM."

It didn't strike Art as the smartest thing his captain had ever done but he knew little more about the workings of Jorf's mind than he did of THEM. If they enjoyed shooting up primitives, perhaps they'd kill each other with equal alacrity.

With Baz on the console and Jorf's unmistakable voice over the PA the *Nishrub* men guarding the tank had THEM on the beltway in something less than a minute.

The THEM commander took in the situation with one glance at the holo.

"Which way you want to die?" Jorf asked.

"I would prefer neither," the THEM commander said. He gave Baz an unfathomable look. The ex-librarian smiled. The THEM commander turned back to Jorf. "My men are hungry."

Jorf nodded at the cook, who began serving the same food to THEM already sitting at consoles. When THEM ate it without protest Jorf relaxed.

So that's how they wiped out our fleet, Art thought as he watched hands flick over keyboards. The pressure of one finger and five thousand men die. The two hundred THEM pips on the holo showed fuzzy ionization outlines as they began converging on the captured flagship. In the lull Art had time to realize the THEM commanders out there had probably listened in on every conversation and understood the situation better than he or Jorf. Then he remembered they had not moved until after he had reported to Earth.

Perhaps with that report of THEM prisoners in the *Nishrub*'s tank . . . It was obvious now that THEM had not counted on an expert defense by the flagship's own crew. When fifty ships flared and disappeared from the holo Art abruptly realized how much larger and better armed this flagship must be. Suddenly, THEM were retro firing, retreating in every direction like the explosion of some tremendous festive firework.

"Again!" Jorf yelled. "Shoot again!"

But the captive THEM had beaten off the attack. So far as they were concerned, it was over. In less than a second the THEM fleet had lost one fourth of its strength. Watching the scatter of retreat, Art realized the battle could have been prevented by warning THEM that the flagship would be defended by its own personnel. But he also knew Jorf would never miss a chance to diminish an enemy.

"What's going on up there? Report immediately!" a voice from Earth shrieked.

Art glanced at Jorf but the grizzled Arab was still trying to coax another salvo out of captive THEM on the consoles. Finally the Arab gave up. Gradually the farthest ships lost their fuzzy ionization outlines as they stopped retro firing. "What'll they do now?" Art asked.

"I'm not a mind reader," Baz said. "I can only tell you what I'd do."

Art waited.

"If you were out hunting rabbits and the rabbits started shooting back, what would you do?"

"I don't know," Art said. "Go home for help, I guess." Suddenly he realized what this meant. "Is it true that you have no faster than light communications?"

"True," Baz said. "Nobody's ever found out how to push a wave form FTL."

"So nobody in your home system knows what's happened yet?"

"Not until one of those ships jumps."

The radio boomed again. "Jorf Ali, captain of the Alliance Ship *Nishrub*, this is a direct order from Alliance HQ. There are enemy ships between you and this base. Earth must be protected at all costs. Bring your ship immediately into cislunar orbit."

They were sufficiently shook up to stop playing code games. Art was not surprised when Jorf ignored the booming voice.

"We follow THEM ships back to your own planet," the Arab said, "and don't give me any bullshit about not having charts."

The THEM commander looked up from his console and waited for Art to interpret. Art rendered Jorf's Arabic into English and still the alien commander stared.

"I told you I'm the only one with any knowledge of Earth languages," Baz said. "You use me as an interpreter. Why do you balk at using a machine?"

Jorf gave an inarticulate growl which Art decided was permission. He nodded and Baz turned on the ship's computer again. Jorf repeated his statement and this time the commander understood.

"Yes," he conceded, "I know where they're going."

"We go first."

"Jorf Ali, report immediately to Earth HQ."

"Tell them go catch their own ship," Jorf growled.

Art had entertained a fugitive hope of going home someday. First Nixon's unpredictable vindictiveness had kept him wandering in foreign climes. Now . . . Assuming they ever really won—could the *Nishrub*'s men ever tread their native soil again? Not if he knew how strained was the quality of mercy among admirals, Art decided.

For once Jorf volunteered a hint of explanation. "Crazy sons of bitches," he growled. "For THEM this ship is worth a hundred Earths." This time the computer dutifully rendered his aside into a booming commentary for Earth HQ to analyze.

There would be time, Art guessed, for victory parades once THEM were finished. But there were still a hundred fifty undamaged ships here, plus Christ only knew how many off filibustering in other systems. If a single THEM got home to spread the word about Earth, the next hunting party would come loaded for bear.

"What kind of a society do you have at home?" Art asked. "You switch sides; these prisoners fire on their own comrades. What'll your people at home say when they learn what you've done?"

"Loyalty is a refuge for small minds," Baz said. "It relieves the conscience of those incapable of thinking out the logical consequence of any action."

Expediency was practical, Art guessed. But justifying it to Mom and Apple-Pie types required an agility which Art knew he didn't possess. He wondered if this was why politicians went in for gallus snapping. The hell of it was that, amoral as Baz's philosophy might be, it had an inbuilt tendency to triumph over the older virtues.

"Jorf Ali, this is the Alliance commander, HQ Earth—"

This time the voice was almost pleading but before Art could hear the remainder of the plea there was another of those odd gravitic flickerings. This time he seemed abruptly upside down. There was an instant of total disorientation as deck and bulkhead coalesced and the universe wavered in and out of some weird non-Euclidean dimension.

It was over as quickly as it had begun and abruptly Art was aware of the wolfish look of captive THEM fading into disappointment as the *Nishrub*'s men landed on their feet with trained rifles.

"You'll never know how close that was," Baz murmured.

"What happened?"

"We jumped."

"Just like that? We're in your home system already?"

"I couldn't guarantee that," Baz said.

"Error!" the THEM commander shrieked. "We are in the wrong system!"

"My festering phallus, it was an error," Baz chuckled. "He just thought he could get away with it." Before the alien could explain, the same bewildering disorientation flickered again. When Art's eyes focused, the first thing he saw was Jorf's alpenstock poised over the violet-haired THEM commander's skull.

"This is it!" the THEM hastened. "Home system. Really, it was an error."

Art wondered if it was the missed meals that had shattered that amused arrogance. Those THEM looking straight into *Nishrub* men's rifle barrels were not amused now. Maybe, Art thought, they were finally realizing what kind of guests they had brought home to track blood all over the rug.

Bercovici fiddled with his console and the air was filled with the same saturation he had picked up on Earth before he had learned how to fine tune THEM radio. "I don't know if it's their home," the engineering officer said, "but this system's certainly populated. Signals coming from three singles and one binary. Looks like we hit the jackpot." Art was startled until he realized Bercovici's suddenly fluent English was really the computer's.

Great! Art thought. *A year ago I was worrying about Vietnam. Now I'm light-years from Nebraska and only facing four planets!* He knew he should be paralyzed with the realization of how far, how many enemies between him and home. But even terror lost its terror after a while. Art was only numb. "Where are we?" he asked.

Baz shrugged. "Home is an elastic term."

"Does it look like home for most of THEM in that fleet that attacked Earth?"

"It looks like it," the alien hedged. Bercovici's fiddling with the radio finally elicited a single thread of two-tone code. Baz smiled. "We're home. I'd know that hand anywhere."

"Hand?" Then Art remembered how old-time telegraphers on Earth could recognize one another's "fist." "But where are we with relation to Earth?"

Baz punched at a console. Finally Art saw that the lenticular clot of brilliant pinpoints must be the Milky Way viewed from outside. One star was pulsating very like the "you are here" spots in the loofah tracery. The alien fiddled again with the console and another star began flashing. "That's probably yours," he said.

"Probably?"

"It's only a machine. It can't overcome incorrect inputs."

The two stars seemed quite close together. Art was about to ask when Baz continued, "Our light-year is based on a planetary period somewhat shorter than yours. I can work it out if you wish but roughly, you're five thousand light-years from home."

To Art the distance seemed less than from Nebraska to the Costa del Sol. He wondered if he would survive the culture shock long enough to see what life was like on another planet, under another star. There was a sudden undulating wail like a dog in pain.

"Flatulent feces!" Baz moaned.

From the sudden flurry Art deduced that something very like the alien's exclamation was about to hit the fan. "Is that a general quarters alarm?" he asked when the wail had ended.

Baz nodded.

"How'd the word get out? Somebody beat us here?"

"I doubt it. The computer probably blabbed its automated head off the instant we completed the jump." He punched the keyboard and their holo duplicated the one Jorf and the THEM commander studied a few meters away. This system seemed crowded. Two binary planets were orbiting the Earth-Moon fashion about a main sequence star whose temperature was slightly whiter than Sol's. The other three usable planets were equidistant in the Trojan points of an orbit somewhat farther out.

"The binary is where life originated," Baz explained. "The rest is artificial."

"You made the planets?"

"Shifted them from their original orbits and did a bit of terraforming. Ah yes, here they come."

Three pinpoints, fuzzy with ionization, began a slow-as-molasses curving out from an orbit between the binary and the Trojan points.

"If, like most primitives, you count on the aid of unverifiable phenomena, now would be an excellent time to invoke them," Baz said.

"I suppose you're beyond all that?"

Baz grinned. "You ought to see us at the race games."

"Anyhow," Art protested, "won't we wipe these three out as easy as we did fifty a while ago?"

"One of those ships is as big and well armed as this flagship, with a full complement trained to defend its home system."

"My strength is as the strength of ten because my heart is pure," Art mused. There was a sudden shock not like those other odd gravitic flickerings.

"*Ahtt!* Tell them sons of bitches in plenty languages," Jorf yelled.

He broke from his reverie to realize Jorf still needed him even though the shipboard computer was handling most of the interpreting now.

"Say bombs already flying. THEM hit us, no way to call back."

"But can't THEM ships outmaneuver a missile?"

"To hell with ships. Four planets gonna turn into asteroids."

"We know," a voice boomed in computer English. "We surrender. Please call back your missiles."

"Call back bullshit," Jorf growled. "Choose quick."

The largest of the three approaching pips flared and went out. A half second later the other two defending THEM blew up. "We got 'em!" Art yelled. Then he realized what had really happened. Perhaps THEM warriors were not so despicably venal as he had thought. He wondered if he would have been capable of this unwavering response if given a choice of Earth's life in return for his own.

"An exceeding dangerous man," Baz said. "A mind befogged with neither education nor sentiment."

Art wondered if it had been a lucky guess. Jorf's capacity for making his own luck seemed unusual. He studied the captive THEM manning consoles, wondering how much and how willingly they had contributed. Another jolt passed through the ship and Art guessed it was the missiles returning to their cradles. "Couldn't those ships have usurped control and diverted them?" he asked.

"Probably ninety per cent of them," Baz said. "If one got through to each planet it would make little difference how many aborted."

"So it's over? Just like that?"

"I doubt it," Baz sighed. Abruptly another pip appeared in the holo. Immediately it flared into oblivion. "That'll be the fleet returning from your system. Unless some of them are smart enough to jump elsewhere and spread the word."

"How can we tell?"

"I imagine the computer will count the flashes for you as they come through. There goes another."

As hours passed Art guessed there might be ways to warn the smaller ships to surrender but he had to admit Jorf's instantaneous destruction of anything that moved was going to prevent future problems. It reminded him uncomfortably of "final solutions" in Earth history. But this time, he reminded himself, the victims had attacked first, had scragged Earth's fleet with the same methodical thoroughness. If THEM and the Alliance had minded their own business, Jorf would still be smuggling arms, content to exercise his genocidal talents against Spaniards.

Finally the computer gave an attention-getting whoop and said, "The last of the Earth invaders has been destroyed."

"Prove it," Jorf growled.

"È veritate," Bercovici said. "I've been keeping my own count."

There was a sudden relaxation as the *Nishrub*'s people finally realized it was really over. Art wondered about the THEM still captive aboard the flagship. Their total lack of amused superiority convinced Art that they knew they were the only survivors, and that this unpredictable Arab would like nothing better than some excuse to make a clean sweep.

The interpreter-computer was balking now, sometimes leaving people to stare blankly in mid-conversation. Art wondered how long it would take before the *Nishrub*'s wound in this immense artificial planet could infect and become terminal. As usual Jorf was ahead of him. "Anybody knows how to work repairs is useful," he said.

Art interpreted into English and while Baz was transmogrifying this latest edict into tonal THEM the interpreter gave a dying gasp and finished the job. The hundred staffers were suddenly brimful with previously undeclared skills. "How many we got altogether?" Jorf asked.

Bercovici fiddled with his console. Unbelieving, he did it again. "Over three thousand," he said.

"You said something about natural selection through volunteers," Art reminded Baz. "What'll happen down there if we turn these prisoners loose?"

"Among thirty billions?" The alien laughed.

The damned computer seemed to have bugged out completely. Jorf used a word Art had never heard before. From context he finally guessed they were going to land and take hostages from the influential citizenry of the five planets below. There was no ambiguity about the rest of the Arab's message. "Then," Jorf continued, "we all gonna have a nice rape."

CHAPTER THIRTEEN

Several days and several thousand annoying details later Art was stepping off a shuttle onto the slightly larger half of the binary. He wondered if he was dressed properly for a rape. "How was it?" he asked a man who had landed forty-eight hours ago and was now returning.

"*Wunderbar! Unheimlich!*" There was an air of dreamy satiation.

Art stepped out into the sounds and smells of a strange planet. The air did not have the cumin, saffron, flowers, and camel-dung stink of the ship. It smelled— Art didn't know what it smelled like. Certainly not Earth. He had been through so many changes of gravity lately that he didn't know whether he weighed more or less than on Earth. For an instant he caught a whiff of what smelled just like tobacco smoke. He studied the crowds. They were neither bustling nor dawdling. He wondered . . .

If the first shift of rapists had kept their part of the bargain, this planet was either amazingly passive or more amazingly blasé. He stared at the beltways and escalators snaking off in every bewildering direction from the shuttle field.

"Good morning, sir. I am to guide you and do whatever I can to make your stay comfortable."

It was the first time Art had ever seen a female alien. Trying not to stare, he wondered how much was artifice and how much of this incredible body was for real.

Like male THEM, she wore shoulder-length violet hair of a straight gloss he had always associated with cheap wigs. Her hairline was slightly higher than he was used to but it seemed genuine. Her brows were unplucked and her eyes seemed curiously small until he realized it was his own reaction to not seeing the heavy make-up every woman on Earth had used for as long as he could remember.

But it was difficult for Art to keep his eyes on hers. His glance kept returning to the mounds of femininity which pointed like twin search-lights, aiming firmly upward-pointing nipples. If his experience with the mammary equipment of Earth females was any guide, Art guessed this one had never borne a child. There was a dewy freshness—as if some sixteen-year-old had just stepped from the incubator.

Like THEM males, she wore skin-tight trousers, this well-filled pair of an orange so brilliant Art suspected it would glow in the dark. Orange boots with moderate heels formed a part of the peg-topped trousers which ended just below a pair of jiggling headlights. *What's wrong?* Art asked himself. *You've never seen a pair of tits before?* No THEM had ever worn a shirt or anything else apart from these peg-topped trouser-boots. He should have expected females to conform. He wondered how a THEM male would react to the unexpected open spaces of a bikini.

The girl smiled, studying him with the same frank interest. Her eyes were of the same violet as her hair. The THEM commander had made some crack about not having time to grow hair. Art wondered what she would look like if she took it off. But mostly, his eyes kept straying back to those incredibly pneumatic, totally nonsagging breasts. Blood rushed to his face. Blood was rushing to other parts of his body. He tried not to stare.

"Perfectly natural," the girl said. "You've been in space a long time. Shall we take care of first things first? We can see the planet afterward."

Art wondered if his suddenly resurrected libido was reading meanings that weren't there. "We'll go to my apartment." She took his hand.

The beltway gave brief kaleidoscopic glimpses of buildings, open spaces, people doing the most astonishing things.

Art felt a sudden suspicion. Was this really home for THEM-Alliance peoples? There seemed a definite possibility that this whole planet was one giant whorehouse. He wanted to ask but . . . He had never yet gotten a straight answer out of a THEM. Suddenly they were off the beltway and the girl was standing on two painted footprints, speaking at a grille. A door slid open with a pneumatic wheeze.

It sounded like she had spoken English to the grille. He considered the possibilities. A planet-wide interpreting computer could prevent misunderstandings. But the bloodiest wars were usually civil, between people who understood one another only too well. To hell with it. Art was more interested in what he and this taut-bodied THEM who smelled faintly of musk were going to do once they got to her apartment.

They passed down a corridor narrower even than those permitted by Spanish building codes and through another door. Art knew he ought to be taking in every detail but he couldn't take his eyes from a pair of things he had seen in countless shapes and colors on Earth. "Shower's in there," the girl said, pointing at a doorway which looked just like a doorway.

Art was unzipping as he tore through it. It was not until he stood naked inside that he saw this was actually quite different from an Earth apartment's bathroom. One of the main differences was that on Earth a pair of arms had never reached out from the wall to hold him motionless. He sensed a spray of mist from some orifice and tried to hold his breath. It was too late. Already he was losing consciousness, beginning to sag within the grip of those mechanical arms.

He awoke on what felt like a water bed. He sat up abruptly, surprised that he was able to move. "Ready?" It was the same soft voice.

"What happened?" Art had never felt this way before. He remembered the only other time he had been under anesthesia, when a Nebraska dentist had removed a superfluous wisdom tooth. For a day afterward he had seen the world through two lengths of pipe. Now he felt—rested, relaxed, refreshed. He must still be floating. Soon it would wear off and he would feel lousy.

"Are you all right now?" She had removed her skin-tight trousers. She had the usual things in the usual places and Art had time to notice that hair colors matched before a wave of total and complete rut overcame him.

She sat on the edge of the bed and when there was no tidal wave Art guessed it was not a water bed after all. He grabbed handfuls of taut young anatomy. Burying his face between those firmly upward-pointing protuberances, he devoted his full attention to doing what comes naturally. They galloped briskly for a minute without moving more than halfway across the bed.

"What happened?" he finally repeated. With an abrupt post-coital clarity he could imagine all sorts of unpleasant possibilities. Half of the *Nishrub*'s men had already made liberty. He wondered if each of them had stepped into a bathroom and been assaulted by a machine. Anything could have happened while he was drugged. He remembered the smiling satiation of returning crewmen. They could be full of post-hypnotic suggestions. They could be full of anything! "What happened?"

"I'm sorry," the violet-haired girl said. "It must have startled you. I should have warned you."

"If you had, I wouldn't have gone in." Saying it, Art knew it wasn't true. Even now only minutes later he felt the return of desire. He was helpless. He had never known this frantic rabbity lust before. He knew though that this alien girl could have anything she wanted from him—information, betrayal—even his own life if that would be the price to burrow once more into her soft and secret places.

"It's—" The girl seemed embarrassed. "You're from a different star," she began. "Even when we travel from planet to planet in this system there are minor upsets." She took a deep breath and Art realized she was reciting a set piece. "Microscopic life, like all life forms, is constantly evolving. But evolution is more rapid in an organism whose life is measured in hours instead of years. It is not a question of sanitation or lack thereof. No superiority is implied, only difference—"

Art smiled at the memory of outraged Americans who refused to believe that Mexican visitors got sick every time they drank New York water. "I'm familiar with the problem," he said. "What'd you do to me?"

"A worming and general clean-out," she admitted.

Something else too. His chest and armpits had been depilated. His close shave seemed closer. But even in the slightly heavier gravity of this binary planet he felt better than he had in months. He wanted to ask her how long he had been unconscious but she leaned over him, brushing his face with those incredible eye magnets. He snapped and soon they were cantering again.

This time it was more leisurely, but still over far sooner than Art considered consistent with his track record. *What's wrong with me?*

"Don't be alarmed," the girl said. "It's a natural reaction. Some cultures have even used it for gathering intelligence."

Art grinned at half-remembered Mata Hari stories, then he remembered a different kind of story—about men in concentration camps who had been held for weeks on the edge of death, expecting any moment to be shot. It had developed to a fine science, this knowing the exact moment when a man would sell his political party, his friends, his soul for the chance to plant his endangered seed. But nobody had asked Art for information—at least he didn't remember anyone asking. "By the way," he asked, "are you speaking English?"

"No. Are you?"

Art stretched, luxuriating in the feel of firm female flesh. Somewhere in the background a soft voice was singing in an odd scale. Lazily he realized her voice had the same rhythm as THEM radio.

> "Kind sir, I beseech thee, think me not immoral.
> "My upbringing's rural, my style's intercrural.
> "I'll crown thee with laurel, bring thee offerings floral,
> "But Malthus be damned, sir, I'll not do it oral!"

Art's companion was bound by no such inhibitions, as he discovered while wondering how a computer could match rhyme and meter. Then he finally understood. The song wasn't in English. The computer's constant help had taught him the alien language.

The girl was teaching him things too. By now Art knew he ought to be tiring. He wondered if his improved stamina was due to the mechanical doctor's ministrations.

Probably. But had the machine cleared up the half-dozen low-grade infections that were a constant part of the human condition, or had he merely been hyped with some inhibition-loosening aphrodisiac? Art found himself doing things he had only read about on the grimy walls of foreign toilets. But the fear, the tension that had been constant since Mediterranean days was oozing away. When he awoke, drained in every sense, the girl gave a happy sigh and caused food to appear.

Aboard the flagship he had always meant to learn something about THEM's table manners but there had never been time. The *Nishrub*'s people ate each after his fashion, some with forks, some with homemade chopsticks, and some with their right hands—all very hurriedly.

The meal which now materialized came with plates to eat from, each with a pair of round, pointed chopsticks such as those he had seen Japanese use, save that these were longer and transparent. The endless profusion of single-mouthful servings made the hundred varieties of *rijsttafel* seem Spartan.

The girl poured something steaming from a Chinese-appearing teapot into tiny translucent cups. Art sipped. A sudden wave of heat, quintessence of mustard and horse-radish unblocked his sinuses. Abruptly he could taste and smell. This, he reflected in startled delight, must be how a dog senses odors. He was ravenous.

The violet-eyed girl flipped an eggcup-sized tureen and something splatted on his plate. It looked like a raw egg with a purple yolk. The girl captured hers with transparent chopsticks and tossed it whole into her mouth. Art tried to catch his. It evaded the chopsticks. He tried again.

My God, he thought, *it's alive!*

The fetal mess struggled up the rim of his plate, slid down and tried again. The girl noticed his discomfiture.

"Good," she said. "Try it."

Art reminded himself that life was relative. Every raw fruit he had ever eaten was alive. Until he had learned they were instant hepatitis he had enjoyed the Mediterranean's raw oysters. He steeled himself and tried again. This time the purple blob lay quiescent between his chopsticks. He tossed it into his mouth.

Art wondered if there were a word to describe an oral orgasm. Would it taste this way if he had not sampled the mind-blowing, sinus-clearing tea first? He had expected something slimy, had steeled himself to overcome a repugnance like the first time he had sampled a raw oyster, but this mouthful was pure mind-blowing bliss. It dissolved, suffused his every sense with a satiation as strong as the gonadial gallops of an hour ago. He was full to overflowing with just one mouthful. How could he ever do justice to the rest of the feast?

The girl sipped that mind-blowing, sinus-clearing drink and indicated for him to do likewise. He did. Immediately the aftertaste was gone. His senses were clear, once more he was hungry. *Going to be trouble,* he knew. *Once a man's eaten of the lotus he'll never go back to ham and eggs.*

She flipped another eggcup-sized tureen onto his plate. This one quivered amorphously for a moment, then crystallized into three gelatinous cubes, each striated with a venous network that reminded him briefly of the loofah tracery of passages aboard the flagship. He captured one of the cubes in his chopsticks. It was crunchy. Then there was an abrupt explosion of flavor as it deliquesced—an unpredictable mélange of chocolate, cinnamon, roast beef, asparagus, all overlaid with a haunting something he remembered—but from where?

"What's your name?" he finally remembered to ask.

"Star."

It took him a moment to realize he was not making an unconscious translation. She had really said "Star." "Jír or jár?" he asked.

"Jérstar."

"What do those 'j' things mean?"

"Jír is a man—a potent male. Jár is an honored old man. Jér is myself, nubile but childless. Júr is a mother." She flipped another eggcup onto his plate. This time it looked like a spoonful of brown rice until he noticed each grain had a tiny tadpole tail. Gamely, he struggled to pick up the mass with his chopsticks. Jérstar made a warning noise and poured more of the mind-blowing tea.

Art thought about the gender indicators, remembering his earlier suspicions. He wondered if there were any taboos in this society. "I notice there are no designations for homosexuals," he said.

"What's that?"

Art tried to explain.

Jérstar gave him a fishy unbelieving look. "How could there be any fun in that?"

"Search me," Art said. He sipped tea and waited until his taste buds were cleared for reprogramming. The rice-sized pollywogs were smooth, with an oily richness that reminded him of the time he had sampled an avocado stuffed with baby eels. "How do you make a living?" he asked.

Once more she was puzzled.

Art tried to explain about work and money. Star's face became more blank. She put a hand in an unexpected place and Art abandoned his economics lesson. It was nearly an hour this time before he gave a final gasp, slept, and woke up to eat some more.

"What else do you do?" he insisted. "How do you fill your days?"

Star didn't understand. They were speaking the same language.

Art wondered if she was being willfully stupid or if it just came naturally. "Where does your food and clothing come from?"

"You saw me use the synthesizer. Are you hungry again?"

"But who pays for it?"

"What is pay?"

Art sighed. "Have you ever wanted something that belonged to somebody else?"

"Why should I?" She oozed closer, rubbing acres of agreeably taut epidermis against him. Art responded mechanically, then finally realized he'd had enough. "Let's see what it looks like outside," he suggested.

Immediately clothing appeared, skin-tight boot-trousers in bright green checks for Star, and a larger black pair. Art's ended snugly just below his armpits. They would be comfortable, he guessed, but he wondered if THEM had ever devised anything as utilitarian as a fly. He wished for a shirt or jacket but he couldn't remember having seen any during his lust-fogged dash from the shuttleport. "I suppose you have weather control too?"

"What's weather?"

Art guessed that answered his question. They went out the narrow hallway into the cloudless skys and brilliant colors of a planet under a different sun. Half anticipating the answers, he asked, "What do you call this planet?"

"The world."

"What do you call the sun? No, don't tell me."

The smaller half of the binary planet turned out to be Number Two. "I suppose those planets out in the Trojan points are Three, Four, and Five?" he asked.

"The largest is Monster Biter. The others are Rutting Woman and Megaphallos."

"You must have some interesting mythology," Art guessed. They got onto a beltway and scenery blurred. Yet he could feel no wind. He put out a hand and encountered no barrier but the beltway slowed.

"You mustn't do that unless you want off," Jérstar said.

"By the way, how long was I knocked out after that ingenious bathroom of yours got hold of me?"

"Twenty hours."

Art tried to remember Baz's indoctrination. That would be about twenty-four Earth hours, he guessed. And he had been indulging his gonadia for how many more? Soon he would have to report back to the captured flagship. He wondered if it had been repaired by now. Would there be time to learn anything about this planet? "What's the one thing every visitor wants to see?"

"There are many. Perhaps the relocation memorial? It commemorates moving the three planets inward and making them livable."

"Exactly the place I don't want to go. How do ordinary people live? What do they fill their days with if nobody knows what work is?"

"Would you like to visit my mother and father?"

Art wondered if there would be any awkwardness. He guessed not, or she wouldn't have offered to take him. "Sounds great."

"Which one first?"

Once more Art knew he had dropped the ball somewhere. "Which would be most interested in meeting a stranger?"

Star gave him an odd look. "My mother," she finally said.

"What's that big round thing we're passing, the one with all those people climbing around the edge?"

He couldn't understand her absent-minded reply.

"Either I didn't get it or the computer's pooped out. What does that mean?"

"Baby place," she said.

That, Art suspected, could mean several things. "By the way," he said, wondering if he was treading on forbidden ground, "you seem a thoroughly healthy young woman."

Star's blank look forced Art to re-examine some of his own taboos. He had meant to say she looked extremely fertile. "What I mean is, do you do something or did that bathroom of yours do something to me?"

Still she didn't understand.

"I'm talking about contraceptives," he said.

"Oh," Star said vaguely. "I don't know. I think it is in the food."

Art still wondered what she meant by "baby place." "We're going to meet your mother?" he asked.

"Yes."

"What exactly do you mean by mother?"

Star gave him an annoyed look. "The same thing everyone means."

"A female like yourself, impregnated as I have valiantly striven over you, who carried a fetus to full term, after which it was delivered naturally?"

"What does all that have to do with motherhood?"

Art sighed. "On my planet there are people who enjoy making things. Some grow vegetables, bake bread, make clothing, wine, or beer. They don't have to do these things but it gives them pleasure. Is there no one on this planet who reproduces in the old-fashioned way?"

"Oh them!" Star sniffed.

"THEM," Art echoed. "—What the hell was that?" He craned his neck to look back at a miles-square sheet of some folded and wrinkled material that was being stretched across the sky. The parts which were taut and flat were of a cyan indistinguishable from the real sky.

Star shuddered. "I don't know why they can't do that at night."

"But what is it?" The girl acted as if it were some gamy but necessary activity like garbage collecting or sewer cleaning. "Do they enjoy doing it? If it's disagreeable, who pays them?"

"Can't we talk about something else?" Star's anguish was so real Art guessed he'd better. He was about to ask what that block-long sausage-shaped thing was doing quivering in great undulating waves in the center of what looked like a park but Star gripped his arm and guided him to a branch off the beltway.

Soon they had slowed until he could see the tiny flowers which lined the beltway. Their mathematical perfection made him wonder if, like Los Angeles, this planet had discovered plastic vegetation. But now she was leading him down a short walk which looked very like concrete. She stood on two blue-painted footprints and spoke into another grille. A door hissed open and they strode down a narrow hallway. He followed Star inside an open door. "This is my mother," Star said.

Art had been ready for anything from a crone to a machine. He saw a girl very like Star, possibly a year or two younger, same violet eyes and hair, with a pair of rose-colored virginal nipples surmounting a matched set of mammaries as phenomenal as her daughter's.

"Impossible!" Art said, and squirmed at the memory of how often he had told this same lie. Only this time there really had to be a mistake. "I'll believe sisters but she's too young to be your mother."

It must have been the wrong thing to say. Star's face crumpled and seemed suddenly much older. Her mother made an inquiring noise. "They were just putting it back as we passed under," Star said.

Mother patted Star's shoulders and murmured phrases Art could guess at without really hearing them. "Perhaps you'd like to use the bath?" Mother asked him.

Oh no, not that again! Then Art realized he had already been deloused. Mother just wanted a moment alone with her daughter. He went into the bath.

"Jírart," Mother called a few moments later, "I'm ready. You can come out now."

"I wish I could," Art yelled. "This goddam machine gave me a bath and now it won't give me back my clothes."

There was a tinkle of laughter. "But, Jírart, nobody wears clothing inside the house."

Art hoped he could keep his cool in the presence of a mother-daughter combination. But when he came out Star was gone. "Where is she?" he asked.

"On her way to a repair center," Mother said. "Now come sit down and tell me about your planet."

The only place to sit was on the bed. Art crossed his legs. Mother sat beside him. He was searching for something to say when she lay back and curled up behind him. From the corner of his eye Art saw two superbly unwrinkled knees edging closer. Then he felt a firm flat belly against his back. An instant later that matched set of mammaries bumped his shoulder blades. Arms snaked around his neck. Enough to turn a man's stomach, Art thought.

So he did.

"My name is Júrgen," she said some time afterward.

Art gave her a quick glance but the violet eyes were guileless. "Are you really Star's mother?" he asked.

"Of course."

Júrgen's nipples were virginal. Her firm flat belly had no stretch marks.

"How old were you when she was born?"

"About fifty."

Art wondered if the local calendar counted binary revolutions as years. It was some such confusion that accounted for Methuselah and other such biblical senior citizens. But Júrgen had done her homework. "That would be nearer sixty of your years," she added.

"Is that usual?"

"About average. My application had been on file for six years."

"Have you any other children?"

Júrgen smiled. "After a certain age one becomes just a trifle bored with the problems of the young."

Art wondered if she knew he was twenty-three. "I seem to have said something wrong," he probed. "Why did Star bug out in such a hurry?"

"It was nothing you said. She needed treatment."

"Because of me? I thought that mechanical monster in the bathroom had removed all the risk from interstellar fornication."

"The sky fell."

Shades of Chicken Little! Then he remembered that miles-wide curtain thing. "Is this sun dangerous? Did I get cooked?"

"Your own sun probably gives off more hard radiation. But you must remember Jérstar is only beginning her life."

What did this smooth-skinned centenarian think he was doing? "Is there any real danger?" he insisted.

"Not if she undergoes therapy."

"What about me?"

Júrgen's face underwent a sudden change. "You seem so human," she said apologetically.

This, Art decided, is how it feels to be black in the United States.

"Your life span is so short it will probably have no effect," Júrgen continued. "If there were any serious damage the bathroom would have warned you."

"How old is Star?"

Júrgen thought a moment. "About a hundred fifty of your years."

Art caught himself speculating how many off-planet strangers she had met, how he compared. He shook his head. From Júrgen's cautious attitude he suspected age was another taboo area. "There are things one doesn't talk about in any society," he said. "The trouble is, they're never the same things."

"You are unusually perceptive," Júrgen said. She thought a moment. "It's difficult. What topics are forbidden on your planet?"

"It depends on what part you come from," Art said.

"How fascinating. You do not all speak the same language and live the same way?"

"Not yet. We came rather close to never doing it."

"You're bitter. Someday you'll understand these things better."

"With my brief and brutal life span?"

Júrgen shrugged and began doing something which made it difficult for Art to remain angry. Was it really possible that she had been born before his great-grandfather had ended a bestial existence in the loft of some Scandinavian freeholder's barn? He struggled to maintain a stiff-necked dignity but the stiffness kept gravitating to a different part of his body. A half hour passed and Art glided gently into a new dimension of sensuality. Eventually, after dozens of feints they grappled for the fall and he lay bemusedly asking himself who had conquered.

"Death," Júrgen said dreamily.

"What?"

"Death," she repeated. "It happens so seldom. We are awkward in its presence. To us it is the ultimate obscenity."

"Make Love, not War."

"Exactly."

"Did you make love to Earth?"

"Yes."

Art remembered those green pips on the holo flaring one by one into oblivion, each flare signaling the extinction of five thousand more humans. "I doubt it," he said.

"What is obscene to you?"

Art tried to sort out what had happened during his lifetime. As a child he had unquestioningly accepted his parents' values. Then Vietnam had forced him to question everything. He remembered the rednecks, contemptuous and secretly envious of the ease with which his generation satisfied their sexuality, never understanding the diversions and sublimations of their own generation's tail-finned cars, their gun collections, their compulsive hunting and fishing. Which was more obscene: a love-in, or the six o'clock news? "I don't know," he said. "I guess death *is* the ultimate obscenity."

Júrgen's look was unfathomable. "He said you were different from the others."

"Who?"

"Járbaz."

"You know him? Is he well known on this planet?" Art wondered if the alien he had captured was something more than a historian-librarian.

Júrgen smiled. "He's Jérstar's father. Also my husband."

"*Ahtt! Ya, Ahtt,* you hear me?"

"Yessir!"

"Come back *Nishrub II,*" Jorf said. "We go home now. You have nice rape?"

"Yeah," Art said. But he suspected it had been the other way around.

CHAPTER FOURTEEN

The shuttle circled the big ship before slipping tail-first into a docking sphincter. Art saw no evidence of the *Nishrub*'s hole in her namesake. He reminded himself to ask what had been done with the wreckage of the old waterboat. Not that he much cared but in his cubicle had been a couple of hundred science-fiction paperbacks. Someday perhaps he could enjoy THEM books but so far he had seen nothing resembling a novel. These aliens seemed to use literacy only for accounting and instruction manuals.

There was a whoosh of equalizing pressure and he was back in the acrid smoke, cookery, camel-dung stink of the flagship. He wrinkled his nose. Number One hadn't smelled like this. He wondered if THEM had doctored up the ship air this way to con the captain or if it was just an effort to make the Arab feel at home.

When he found his way to the bridge Jorf and the THEM commander were haggling over last-minute details. "Allo, Ahtt," the Arab said absently. "Call muster."

Art did. The *Nishrub*'s men had been a lean and hungry band of misfits. Now each man seemed kilograms heavier, reposed. Art remembered the hours he had been unconscious after that machine in the bathroom. He hoped they weren't all walking time bombs. Moonface was happier than ever but liberty on a strange planet had done nothing for his IQ. There were twenty men unaccounted for. Art wiped his neck and went through it one more time. There were still twenty men missing. He called Jorf.

"Yah, I forgot. They're staying in this system. McQuoyd and Nessim staying too."

That left Art to handle everything. He supposed he ought to feel honored. He went through the roster again, separating the quick from the dead. Finally it looked right.

There was an ululation like a dog with his tail under a rocking chair and gravity flickered crazily. When Art's heart settled down he realized they had jumped again. He punched at a console and saw something very like the solar system. They seemed to be viewing it about thirty degrees above the ecliptic. Earth and Mars were in conjunction on the far side.

"What'll happen if I take a ship this big into cislunar orbit?" Jorf asked.

"To the ship?" the THEM commander asked.

"To hell with ship. What about tides?"

The THEM frowned and punched a console. "Better stay out somewhere beyond the binary," he said. "I hadn't realized your planet had so much water."

Baz drifted in. "Have a nice time on Number One?" he asked.

"Yes, thanks," Art said. "But I would have liked to see more."

"At your age planets are for pleasure. You can learn all you want from the library."

"*Ahtt!*" Jorf was making signs at Bercovici. The engineer nodded. Jorf caught Art's arm and led him into a cubicle. "We can talk here," he said in Arabic. "Berkóvich has turned off all those things your Mr. Nixon is so enamored of. Now tell me what you saw down there."

"Didn't you go ashore?"

Jorf gave him a level look and Art realized he should have known better. He tried to recall what little he had learned. Mostly he seemed to remember violet-hued pubic hair.

Jorf was silent for a while. "This woman called herself Baz's wife?"

"And daughter," Art added.

"How do you feel since that thing put you to sleep?"

"Fine. I'm worried, of course. I don't know how much is really possible with all this post-hypnotic jazz."

Jorf grunted. There was a moment of silence, then he said, "You good boy. We go to Earth now."

"Everybody?"

"Just you and me."

"Who's going to mind the store?"

"Berkóvich found a way to make people sleep."

"That sounds more like the pharmacist's line."

"Not drugs," Jorf explained. "The engineer found a machine."

"Do THEM know about it?"

"It's their ship."

"I mean do they know *you* know and that you're going to use it?"

Jorf shook his head.

They went back to the bridge. Bercovici was superintending as THEM worked the ship into translunar orbit and readied a shuttle. Art wanted to ask how the soporific worked but the engineer was too busy. Nor did he feel quite right about asking Baz. But the alien had taught him how to use the library. He began punching a vacant console.

Jump Emergency Backup. Warning: *JEB does not prevent aging but can be used to slow metabolic processes by a factor of* 10^{10}. *Repeated use shortens life expectancy less than 1% in the first millennium. Note: Use after this age creates dramatic and sometimes irreversible—*

At first Art thought it was some kind of glorified deep freeze, then he discovered that THEM used an electro-magnetic field to decelerate molecular motion, thus avoiding problems with ice crystals during defrosting.

"*Ahtt!*"

Hastily he turned off the console. When he turned Baz stood behind him. If the librarian had seen, he gave no sign.

After a couple of days on Number One and a few hours in the *Nishrub II*'s now flickerless gravity Art was half nauseated during the hours of near zero grav before the shuttle turned off its ion rockets and shifted to atmospheric chemicals. They landed without fanfare at Bolling Field. Art still wore his peg-topped THEM pants. When he saw the chill mist outside he grabbed a tanker jacket.

Jorf had shown more foresight. Over the years-out-of-style business suit he always put on for special occasions, he wore a cheap unlined *djellaba* of scratchy wool. "Colder than Casablanca," he muttered, as he pulled the peaked hood over his graying bullet head. Art tried to hold his breath.

Finally he had to breathe. For a moment he thought he was going to vomit all over the walkway. The combined stench of diesel, cheap tobacco, decaying food, all overlaid with a damp odor of mildew and ancient fish—had Earth always smelled like this? They caught a taxi.

The cab driver had lived in Washington since WWII and didn't turn a hair at their appearance. Art pulled his neck down into the tanker jacket and tried to see where they were. There was too much mist on the windows. He gave up and tried to ignore his lurching stomach. The guard at the Pentagon had not been born until ten years after WWII. He turned several hairs. Looking at the flustered child, Art suddenly realized he was growing old—almost twenty-four.

Jorf lost patience and turned up his radio. "Berkóvich," he growled, "tell these copulators with chacma that if the commander of the Alliance fleet is not permitted to give his report here, he'll go to some planet where he's appreciated." He squatted by the doorway, drawing the skirt of his *djellaba* over sockless sandaled feet.

The eighteen-year-old guard panicked. "How about you?" he asked Art. "Can you speak English?"

"Only when it suits me," Art said, and squatted beside the Arab. It annoyed him. Jorf's English wasn't all that bad. Besides, Art was nervous about other things. As a member of the Alliance he was immune to reprisals from purely national governments, but strict legality had never been a strong point with the law-and-order administration which still mismanaged this demoralized country.

An elderly man in a naval uniform with gold braid up to the elbows came bursting from the entrance. "Captain Ali!" he exclaimed. "Why didn't you tell us you were coming? We could have arranged a welcome. Don't you know the whole world is waiting to see you? Earth could use a hero right now. We could have arranged for TV coverage, the whole thing."

"That's why," Jorf said. "Where do I make my report? I've got to get back to my ship."

The radio Jorf wore somewhere inside his *djellaba* had carried easily enough back to the *Nishrub II* but Art saw that for some reason the interpreter was not working down here. He translated Jorf's remarks into English.

"Ah, you must be the ship's Talker. Jansen, isn't it? Newscasts've been full of you these last two days."

Oh Jesus! Art thought. By now they had probably dug up the whole bit. Every flag-waving red-neck in the country would be persecuting his blameless parents for failing to drown this abomination along with the rest of the litter.

"You *are* Arthur Jansen, aren't you?"

"I'm the ship's Talker," Art said. "My captain doesn't have much time." *Or patience,* he mentally added.

For an impromptu reception it seemed tremendously red carpet to Art. A mixed bag of admirals and generals with Alliance badges pinned onto dozens of national uniforms formed a respectful audience as Art delivered a report of their capture of the *Nishrub II* in paragraph-long spurts. From the amusement and horror on some faces Art knew that at least some small part of the audience, including a one-eyed man in tanker uniform, was understanding Jorf's original unexpurgated version. Suddenly Art realized who the one-eyed man was. Jorf, apparently, had known all along. A fathomless look passed between them.

There were, it seemed to Art, entirely too many admirals and generals in outmoded uniforms here. Something had happened to the Alliance's recruiting system. Finally Jorf's report was over and the audience crowded forward. Art wondered how long he would put up with this adulation from the sort of men he despised. But the Arab was actually smiling. Alliance-Pentagon interpreters mixed with the crowd and Art took advantage of the respite to guzzle a gin and tonic. A man in civilian clothing cornered him and extended a mike. "Lafferty from UP," he said. "Would you care to say something for the public?"

"I just did."

The newsman put away his mike. "I caught a very odd expression on your face when you were up there doing your language thing," Lafferty said. "I wondered if you were thinking what I think you're thinking."

Jorf seemed to be enjoying himself tremendously. Art tried to remember the last time he had seen that fatuous smile. "I'll give you an exclusive," he told the newsman, "if you'll fill me in first on what happened here."

"Fair enough," Lafferty said. "Just before the battle the Alliance ambassador and all the rest of them took off to warn some other system. Before the launching pad was cold the old guard started reorganizing. Oh, nothing spectacular but the Old Boy Network pulled a transfer here and there and before you knew it all the Alliance selections were out there pulling space duty. And down here the Chairbourne Command is doing business as usual."

"I see," Art said. "What do you suppose they have in store for my captain?"

Lafferty gave a sour grin. "Apart from the gold watch and the handshake?"

Art had wondered why Jorf had not been anxious to return for a hero's welcome. He glanced back where admirals and generals crowded to pat the Arab's back while uniformed messmen plied him with cocktails and cigars. Jorf was grinning like a monk in a whorehouse. Then his eyes met the one thoughtful eye of the slight man in tanker uniform. It seemed to Art that neither of these two was trying to fool the other.

"If there anything else you'd like to know?" Lafferty hinted.

"Is there anything else I ought to know?"

"I don't think so."

"All right," Art said. "The Alliance and THEM don't exist separately. It's all the same."

Lafferty was neither shocked nor unbelieving. "Smart money began to suspect that about the time the Alliance ambassador bugged out," he said. "I suspect those clowns over there kissing your captain's ass have known it for some time. They've just been trying to come up with some version to keep the egg off their own faces."

"Will they let you tell the story?"

Lafferty gestured behind him where a battery of cameras was capturing the scene. "Nothing gets out of here live," he said. "They go over the film pretty well but I've got your face on film and your voice on tape. Once they clear the film I can lip sync your voice back onto it. You'll come through loud and clear on the six o'clock news."

"Wait," Art said.

"How long?"

"Is there any way I can get in touch with you?"

Lafferty slipped him a card with a number on it.

"I'll let you know," Art said. "Meanwhile, if Jorf or I disappear or seem to be making any odd-sounding public statements . . ."

"*Tu irais loin,*" Lafferty said unexpectedly, and punched him on the shoulder.

"*Ahtt!*"

"Yessir!" Art guessed it would do no harm to hint that Jorf ran a tight ship.

Jorf handed him a fistful of money. "Your radio working?"

"Yessir."

"Okay. Go enjoy yourself. I'll call you when I need you."

Lafferty watched interestedly. Art wondered if this perceptive man spoke Arabic too. The newsman muttered something into his lapel mike and an instant later somebody began having trouble with the floodlights that illuminated half of the conference room. While admirals and generals offered advice and jockeyed to pose closest to Jorf the newsman helped Art ooze quietly out into the corridor.

"I guess I ought to get a change of clothes," Art said.

"Only if you want to. Those things you're wearing are suddenly *in*."

"Oh?"

"There's a quiet bar out the way you came in and about nine blocks left. It has a phone."

"Why a phone?"

"If you really want to relax you'd better not be seen too much with me."

"Right," Art said. They went out unchallenged and walked in opposite directions. On the way to the bar Art saw a phone booth. He put his hand in his pocket and then remembered Jorf had given him only bills. He tried to think of some way to call the operator but he hadn't seen an American dime for over a year and a half. Then, standing indecisive in front of the phone booth, he saw one on the sidewalk. He wondered if it was an omen. "I want to call Nebraska," he told the operator. "Ask if they'll accept the charges."

"Arthur. I've been waiting to hear from you. Everyone's been most eagerly waiting."

What the hell? Mom never talked like this. Abruptly Art knew what was happening. "You all right? Are they leaving you alone?"

"Your father and I are fine. Initially there were problems. Bert, Uncle Gus, Gregory, Edgar, and Dan all send their love."

"I see," Art said. "Things are a little better now. Could I send you some money?"

"No, we're all right that way," Mom said. "When are you coming home?"

"I don't know. I'll let you know."

"Take your time. Get it all out of your system."

Art hung up. He had never realized Mom had such a talent for intrigue. He had never heard of Bert, Uncle Gus, Gregory, Edgar, or Dan. He grinned at the knowledge that somewhere somebody was gritting teeth in impotent rage as he strung initials together. Walking on toward the bar, he pondered what Mom had meant about getting out of this system.

It was still misty and growing dark now. He had never been in Washington before. Where the hell was the Pentagon? He remembered stories about muggings in the capital and wished he had some kind of weapon. Finally he saw it.

The bar was warm and dimly lit. He studied the bewildering array of bottles and asked for a beer. Nobody else paid him the slightest attention. When he saw the clothes some of the others were wearing he knew why. "Is this place gay?" he asked.

The man behind the bar gave him a startled glance. "You from out of town? Lately even the straight crowd dresses that way." The bartender glanced at Art's skin-tight boot-trousers. "No," he said in a different voice, "you're in the wrong place."

"Relax. I came by these clothes honestly." Immediately Art wished he hadn't said it but the barkeep was busy serving somebody else.

"Hello, you're new around here, aren't you?"

The blonde was built of the stuff dreams are made of. She reminded him of those lovely lissome Swedish girls from whose bones he had helped warm the winter in Málaga. But . . .

Though it had been a while, Art didn't think he had completely forgotten the art of picking up girls in bars. He wore a grease-smudged tanker jacket which someone had abandoned in the shuttle. His peg-topped THEM trouser-boots were drab amid the resplendent glitter of the bar's other patrons. Art looked down on his luck. The blonde in the slit lamé skirt didn't look motherly.

"I'm just a poor homeless boy," he sighed, "suffering from a terminal case of atrophied gonadia."

To his total lack of surprise she didn't bug off. "Use it or lose it," he explained. "One of the basics of natural selection. Of late I cast longing looks on boys and sheep."

"Poor dear," she purred. "Would you like to freshen up in my shower?"

"Did I mention that I have a loathsome disease and am also broke?"

The blonde laughed. She really had the equipment and Art knew he would have been less immune if it had not been for a mother-daughter combine some hours ago under a different star. Lafferty hadn't had time even if he had decided to ignore their agreement. Then Art remembered some brass hat had said the newcasts were full of him. His enlistment in the Alliance had spun no cameras. Probably they had cobbled footage of him from old photos, home movies, college records.

This blonde wasn't going to give up. Art guessed it was as good a way as any to kill time until Jorf needed him. Leaving the bar with her, he remembered the look that had passed between Jorf and that Israeli general.

"Shower's in there," the blonde said. By now he had learned to call her Iris. Remembering the last couple of strange bathrooms, Art was cautious. He wasn't expecting mechanical arms but Earth was fully capable of closed circuit cameras or just plain goons. When the bathroom turned out to be nothing but a bathroom he gratefully showered. "Be with you in a minute," the blonde promised, going in as he came out. When her minute was up she found Art in bed with the covers pulled up to his chin. This neither shocked Iris nor annoyed her. She did feel somewhat put-out when she learned he was asleep.

CHAPTER FIFTEEN

A couple of hours later Art awoke refreshed and willing to try a quick grapple. Iris sat across the room wearing a negligee which exposed great grabbable lengths of thigh. She was painting her nails and trying to hide her annoyance. "Feeling better now?" she asked.

"Much better." Art yawned his way into the bathroom and discovered a still-packaged toothbrush. It was a thoughtful touch, he decided.

When he came out she had prepared instant coffee. Art had never cared much for coffee until he had gotten to Spain and learned what *café con leche* properly made in an espresso machine could taste like. One of travel's greatest disappointments had been his discovery that Morocco, though Arab, was freaked on mint tea and that *café au lait* there was likely to be boiled milk with only the faintest hint of brown. He sipped Iris's instant enema in line of duty.

"It must have been exciting up there," she began.

"You know how space is—months and months of boredom. I could have used somebody like you up there." He accented the wrong syllable in "somebody."

"Did you kill lots of THEM?"

"A few. What's been going on here? Did they bomb you?"

"Mostly out in the country. It seemed almost as if they were trying to miss us. Were THEM as mean as everybody says?"

"They didn't have to wipe out our fleet, did they?"

"What do you mean?"

"If they'd shot up a couple of ships to demonstrate how hopeless it was, the whole thing could've been settled without killing every man on Earth with gumption enough to defend it." Suddenly he realized the blonde's pursuit of him might be totally innocent. Washington had never been oversupplied with men. Now maybe the whole planet was short of hot-blooded studs.

"But once you got moving, you didn't take any prisoners, did you?"

"We took more prisoners than THEM." Iris, Art decided, was about as innocent as the Alliance ambassador. She twisted in her chair, managing to expose another few centimeters of thigh.

Art reached for it but she was suddenly coy. He put down the lousy coffee and began looking for his clothes.

"You're not leaving?"

"Just remembered something important."

"Can't it wait?" The negligee gaped more invitingly. She came up behind him and put her arms around him.

"It could," Art said. He kept on climbing into his peg-topped pants. *Sonofabitch!* He began searching frantically. His radio was gone! "Can I use your phone?"

"It's out of order."

Art tried and it was. "See you later, maybe." He rushed from the apartment. There was a phone in the lobby. He found the dime the operator had returned when he phoned his mother.

"Lafferty?"

"Where the hell have you been? That wild man of yours has been screaming for you to come back up to the ship for over an hour!"

"Is there any way you can let him know I'm coming?"

"Yeah. Everything's tied into one board now. The shuttle's waiting out at Bolling. But what about that other matter?"

"Wait'll I'm on my way."

"You sound scared."

"I am."

"Where are you?"

Art told him.

"I'll pick you up."

Art nearly dived for the shrubbery before he realized the slowing car was Lafferty. "What the hell's been going on?" he asked.

"What happened to your radio?"

"I might have lost it but I suspect an entirely too available blonde had something to do with it."

"Oh?"

"I get the distinct impression that somebody's trying to dig up evidence for a war crimes trial," Art said. "I'm a draft dodger and my hair's too long but I just don't fancy joining Lieutenant Calley."

"You could always claim you were just following orders."

"Where's Jorf?"

"Up on the ship, I guess. They took him in hook, line, and sinker."

"That I doubt. What'd they do?"

"Assembled a crew of experts to take the ship apart. Everybody who could pull rank crowded into the shuttle too. So many they had to send down two more boats."

"What makes you think they're going to do him dirty?"

"If they're just going up there to congratulate Captain Ali instead of relieving him of his command, why didn't they let any newsmen go along?"

"I see," Art said, though he really didn't.

Lafferty sighed. "A week ago we had world government. Now the only thing that held it all together has disappeared. Everything's up for grabs. Is that ship really as big as a planet?"

"Big as a rather small one," Art said absently.

Lafferty piloted his Buick confidently through the mist. Art hadn't the faintest notion of where he was. He dozed and started awake. How could he be sleepy at a time like this? He wondered if it was the gravity or if he was suffering a reaction from whatever Jérstar's bathroom had done to him. Suddenly they were at Bolling.

A guard shined his light into the car and compared a picture in his hand with Art. When Lafferty flashed his press pass the guard waved them on through. Lafferty parked the Buick a hundred meters from the shuttle and they hurried to the ramp. Art looked up. The pilot was the blue-eyed man who spoke bad French and worse Arabic.

"Hey, you can't go aboard!" a guard yelled at Lafferty.

"You want to?" Art asked.

"Are you out of your skull? Of course I do!"

"Wir kommen die beide an Bord," Art yelled.

The blue-eyed man nodded. He held an automatic weapon cradled in his arms. The guard on the ground stopped running. Thirty seconds later they were lifting off.

"How long'll it take to get there?" Lafferty asked.

Art relayed the question to the blue-eyed man, who shrugged. "Ask Bercovici," he said. "He's piloting us."

"I wondered when you'd learned to fly these things."

"I'm just here to make sure the right people get on or stay off."

"What's going on?"

"*Sais pas.* Did they try to buy you?"

"What?"

"First one wanted to know if Jorf runs a tight ship."

Art waited.

"For a hundred dollars I told him yes."

"The first one?" Art repeated.

"The next guy offered me five hundred to kill Jorf."

"What'd you say?"

"I told him a man that tough ought to be worth a thousand."

"Did he—?"

The blue-eyed man at the pilot's console waved a fistful of money.

Art fiddled with the radio. He caught odds and ends of talk from crewmen who still wore the radio parts of their suits. Their conversation sounded oddly stilted through the interpreter. "Does Jorf know I'm coming?" he asked.

"*Später,*" Bercovici said. "I'm busy landing you now."

The shuttle backed into a docking sphincter and a moment later Art felt the tiny pressure change as doors opened into the ship. "Jesus!" Lafferty whooshed, "what's that?"

Art had gotten used to it but after a spell on Earth he had to admit the stench of camel dung, smoke, the herbs and spices of Arab cookery was all a little overpowering. "I'm not sure," he said. "I suspect it started out as psychological warfare but it didn't work. I'll remind the old man to see about changing it."

Art noticed captured THEM roaming freely about the bridge. For an instant he wondered if there really had been something done to the *Nishrub* men's brains during that liberty on Number One. Then he realized nothing much had happened to him. And Jorf had never left the ship. Baz appeared. He looked old and tired. "You're in for interesting times," the alien said. "Remember regrets are nonproductive."

"What do you mean?"

"That day you caught me in the shower. It wasn't entirely an accident."

"Oh?" If the alien had been listening in on suit radio, he must have recognized a kindred spirit in Art. But what else had he recognized? "Where's Jorf?"

"Your captain is rather busy at the moment."

Art turned on the aged librarian. "Just for once, no bullshit please. What the hell's going on?"

"A series of arrests. Something to do with failure to engage the enemy."

Bercovici was still manning the console. Other *Nishrub* men mingled with THEM performing routine tasks. Art wondered if Jorf was going to be the scapegoat. "They'll never make it stick," he said. "They should have tried it the other way around and racked him for massacring prisoners."

Baz gave him an odd look. *"They,"* he said pointedly, "probably would have. But your captain has arrested the entire general staff. An exceeding dangerous man."

"Ahtt!"

"Yessir!" It was funny. Art had always been afraid of the unpredictable Arab, even though Jorf had never showed him anything but kindness. But in the Mediterranean, even aboard the *Nishrub,* Art had always managed a bantering informality. Lately . . . not only was Jorf an exceeding dangerous man, he decided, in days to come he might be an exceeding important man.

Jorf signaled Bercovici. The engineer nodded and Jorf led Art into the same debugged compartment. "Why didn't you answer?"

Art told him about the blonde and the missing radio. "I think they're out to get you," he said unnecessarily. "By the way, where's all the Pentagon brass?"

"Asleep."

"There wasn't room for them and THEM?"

"We need THEM to run the ship."

"Can you trust THEM?"

"Can I trust anybody?"

"People on Earth may not like this."

"Tomorrow we go back down. You'll help me talk."

"Why not talk up here? You've got them all."

"To hell with these uniformed clowns. We talk to UN."

"Why me? They have interpreters."

"I think you understand me better."

Art wondered if he understood this mystifying man at all. "Is it safe? If they catch you away from the ship again—"

"Berkóvich stays. Anyhow," Jorf continued, "we got to go. I talk from up here people say, 'That goddam Arab think he's God.'"

Jorf was the last man Art had ever expected to understand the democratic touch. "What're you going to say?"

The aging bullet-headed man sighed. "I wish I was fishing. What month is it?"

"February, I guess."

"Sardines soon." The Arab's eyes flickered. "Why wars?" he asked.

It was Art's turn to shrug. "Not enough to go around," he guessed. "But mostly, I think it's boredom."

"Or maybe just too many people."

Art felt a thrill of fear. This was the most powerful man in the world talking. He hoped Jorf didn't mean what it sounded like. He was going to ask but the Arab stood up. The conference was over.

Art wandered down to the galley and scrounged a meal. It was as good as anything he had ever tasted on Earth but he knew Earth food would always seem drab now that he had tasted . . . He wondered if the other *Nishrub* people had tasted the same food on Number One. He was afraid to ask. Baz had arranged a special reception for him. Maybe the others hadn't sampled the gustatorial delights available. If Earth ever found out—if there was no way to make enough to go around . . . Art choked down his meal and decided it was a secret he dared share with no one. He went back to his compartment and to bed. It was a long time before he went to sleep.

When he woke the blue-eyed man was manning Bercovici's console. "Do you know what you're doing?" Art asked.

"I'm learning. They do most of the work." He pointed at THEM manning similar consoles.

"What were you before you joined up?"

"A soldier."

"Why does anybody want to be a soldier?"

The blue-eyed man gave him a look surprisingly like Jorf's. "If you eat meat," he said, "don't sneer at the butcher."

Art sighed. Life would be equally impossible without garbage men, he guessed. Somewhere in this ship were the hostages from Number One. Remembering the mates and twenty men back on Number One, Jorf had not wanted to mistreat the hostages but they, along with the several thousand captured THEM were a constant danger. The problem was solved in an unexpected way as Art was leaving the bridge. A hostage THEM was in the lounge making faces as he sampled coffee for the first time. "You actually drink this stuff?"

"Some of us even like it," Art said.

The THEM changed the subject. "You have the captain's ear?"

"As well as anybody," Art guessed. He wondered how much he would be offered to murder—

"Could you ask him when we can be permitted to sleep?"

"Is somebody stopping you?"

"You didn't even process the POWs until a few hours ago," the hostage said accusingly.

Suddenly Art understood what kind of sleep the hostage was talking about. "You *want* to be put in storage?"

The THEM took a deep breath, then controlled himself. "See one primitive planet, you've seen them all. I was never much of a tourist to begin with."

"But you'll be out of touch," Art protested. "Everybody—your friends and family—when you get back to your own planet—"

The THEM's amusement was tinged with pity. "If we aged as quickly as primitives it might be catastrophic," he agreed.

"I'll see what I can do," Art promised.

Jorf was amused too. "Too goddam many strangers running around my ship. Put them away."

It took Art most of the next four hours. Looking at the morguelike tiers of deactivated bodies, Art reflected that a man's attitudes, everything about life would be different if he lived forever. What difference would twenty or a hundred years away from family or friends mean if they would all be the same age when he returned? Probably, Art guessed, in that kind of a culture they'd all still be driving the same old car or whatever its THEM analogue might be. He wondered if styles ever changed.

Bemused, he wandered about the tiny part of the ship that was familiar. In the lounge where they had captured the THEM skipper the pharmacist had fiddled with the hot drink machine until it emitted something very like the *café con leche* Art had longed for since Spain.

"By the way," the Spaniard said, "your friend's sick."

"What friend?"

"That THEM you snagged coming out of the shit tank. I put him to bed in there."

Art put down his coffee and went into the improvised sick bay. Looking old and drawn, Baz lay face up. Art thought he was asleep but the alien's lips moved. "Not your fault," he said in a voice like rustling leaves.

"What's wrong? How come you're not zonked out like the others? Oh, Jorf woke you up along with those staffers that're helping run the ship?" Suddenly Art knew what was wrong. *Repeated use shortens life expectancy less than 1% in the first millennium. Use after this age creates dramatic and sometimes irreversible—*

"Why didn't you say something?" he asked. "I could have talked him into keeping you out of—what can I do? There's got to be something. How old are you?"

"Too old."

"But why? You're a professional coward just like me. You told me so yourself."

"I've also lived too long. After a certain age one becomes just a trifle impatient with the problems of the young."

Art tried to remember where he had heard that phrase before. "I'm young," he said.

"You're also, apart from myself, the only sane person aboard this ship."

"What are you *really?* My reception on Number One was too well organized to have come from some old sorehead feuding with the government."

"One of us on every ship," Baz said. "You might say we are the real commanders."

"Then why didn't you command?"

Baz coughed and had trouble catching his breath. "What was the alternative? It was an immoral war but it's also immoral to turn those thugs loose on my own plànet. It seemed to me that Earth was better equipped to deal with them—an opinion which events have proven correct."

"You could have taken them beyond the three-billion-mile limit and blown them up," Art said.

"Instead of which we brought Earth a new technology to solve your energy crisis and gain a breathing space. Who knows, you may even survive to join us."

"*Ahtt!*"

"I've got to go now," Art said. "I'll see you later."

"I doubt it." Baz's smile was serene and untroubled.

Art was silent all the way down to Earth. Jorf was always silent. The blue-eyed crewman sat at the console, hands following through on the remote control as he taught himself how to skip a shuttle into the atmosphere. This time they landed in a corner of Kennedy.

Though he had prepared himself against the unexpected Earth-stink his stomach was lurching uncontrollably. He held a handkerchief over his mouth and tried not to breathe deeply.

A limousine pulled up and he guessed somebody had warned the airport they were coming. Then he realized that with both the Moon and cislunar bases destroyed any shuttle had to be from the *Nishrub II*. The people lining New York streets for a glimpse of him and Jorf must know how unique they were. Out of the millions of fighting men recruited from Earth, the *Nishrub*'s people were the only survivors—if one discounted Pentagon drones.

The limousine approached the slab-sided UN building and they were hurried through corridors. As Art surveyed the crowded galleries he wondered for the first time about stage fright. "The mikes'll pick you up direct," he suggested. "You won't gain anything by my being here."

"I talk to you, you say it in English," Jorf said.

And later somebody can always blame my translation. But Art knew he was being unfair. Jorf had never let down one of his own. Perhaps that was why the *Nishrub*'s people had not hesitated to obey him instead of that gaggle of chairbourne blusterers who had come to take over. Art took a deep breath and prepared to address the United Nations.

CHAPTER SIXTEEN

"War's over," Jorf began. "Everybody go home." He paused while Art interpreted. Nobody in the audience seemed inclined to go home.

"All wars are over," Jorf continued. "Anybody starts trouble gonna get plenty."

"Aggression will no longer be permitted," Art interpreted. "The Pax Americana, which could have been enforced in 1945, had it not been for a Cincinnatus complex combined with laziness, has now been supplanted by the Pax Arabica. For the foreseeable future the balance of terror is ended." He glanced at Jorf. The Arab's eyes were hooded but he didn't disagree. After a moment he murmured, "Go ahead."

Art took a deep breath and tried to guess what was on the grizzled man's mind. To his surprise he saw the one-eyed general with the Israeli delegation. One man at least had not been fool enough to go sight-seeing. Jorf was returning the one-eyed man's stare. Art hoped he was guessing right. "Arab nations take heed. The Pax Arabica will tolerate *no* aggression from *any* source. Retaliation will be instant, total, and without benefit of wrangling or boards of inquiry."

"You good boy," Jorf muttered. "Too goddam many people. Anybody wants children got to . . ."

Art interpreted automatically, half taking in what he was saying. Then abruptly he realized Jorf was committing political and probably physical suicide. The galleries rustled and the august personages on the assembly floor exchanged incredulous glances as Art tried to render Jorf's pungent Arabic into English euphemisms. "The world changes and if we are to survive we too must change." He struggled for time to put it all together.

The noise from the floor was getting louder. To Art it seemed that the delegations from countries which had not existed ten years ago, which now existed only through the apathy of their former owners, were making most of the noise. He struggled to present Jorf's program with some kind of coherence. Only the Israeli seemed to be giving him undivided attention. The Americans were passing notes back and forth. The Soviet Union representatives were arguing and shooting black looks at the Chinese. Art glanced at Jorf. The Arab seemed unmoved.

Art was not. "Goddamit!" he yelled, "shut up! Any more noise out of you freeloaders and cloture will be permanent!"

There was a sudden shocked silence. Jorf gave the faintest hint of a smile. Art glared at his suddenly attentive audience.

"This is humanity's last chance. There isn't any vacant real estate out there so we've got to fix up this old place. Revolutionary governments always promise new schemes, which invariably turn out worse than the old. We claim this right. Unlike past reform movements, we have a few advantages. Thanks to Alliance-THEM technology, the energy crisis is over. What we do *not* have is room to live.

"Consumerism is hereby ended. Those who wish to work will be paid. Those who do not will be fed and clothed. Every item of free food and drink will be dosed with contraceptives. Pregnancy will be achieved only when both partners have abstained from freeloading for several months. Clean food, I promise, will be horribly expensive. Inheritance taxes will be one hundred per cent. There will be no procreating poor on this planet. There will be no irresponsible parents. There will be no unwanted children."

Art listened to himself, wondering where all this was coming from. Jorf must have been digging in THEM's library too. He grabbed a ragged breath and continued, "My captain reminds you that cloture is in effect. At an appropriate time elections will be held. Only those paying their own way will vote."

"You good boy. Now we get back to ship quick," Jorf muttered. Art almost repeated it in English before he realized Jorf was through talking. They were nearly out of the building before the numbed General Assembly began emitting roars of outrage. A hook-nosed man in *agal* and *kuffieh* came tearing down the corridor. *"Ya ibn yezidi!"* he shrieked.

Jorf ignored the insult. The Arab delegate in *agal* produced a pistol from beneath his robes and fired one shot. Without realizing what he was doing, Art jumped in front of Jorf. Jorf had a gun in his hand and belatedly Art realized he was spoiling his captain's aim. He wondered if he would live long enough to do something right.

There was a burst of automatic fire. The would-be assassin crumpled and blood gushed from his mouth. Art turned and saw what he had thought was a machine gun was only a pistol in competent hands. The one-eyed Israeli was holding the pistol out butt-forward. Jorf gave the Israeli a nod.

All the way back up to the ship Art was in shock. What on Earth had gotten into him to step between the Arab and a bullet? He wondered if he was losing his mind. And then . . . where the hell had Jorf gotten all those weird ideas? People from all over Earth had been watching that UN session. They weren't going to remember the Arab who had stood in the background quietly moving his lips. The man who was going to be remembered and blamed for all this cockeyed utopianism was Art Jansen, professional coward and freeloader! "Sheeeeeeeeeiiiiiiiiiiittttttt!" Art moaned.

"Ay?"

"I was just wondering," Art stalled. "What does it mean, the thing that guy called you before the Israeli shot him."

"Ya ibn yezidi?"

"You son of a *what?*"

"Yezd. Not bad people. Just stupid. Live in mountains. Worship devil. *Melek taos."*

Brass peacock? Then Art knew he meant the Jebel Druse. They hadn't been stupid enough to align themselves with the Arabs against Israel. But every God-fearing Moslem had despised them since the days when Jews were counselors and physicians in the courts of the caliph.

"That speech you made today," Art said. "They're going to blame me."

Jorf shrugged. "You were Talker on the *Nishrub.* Now you're Talker for the planet."

Suddenly Art saw exactly what he was. This was Harún er Rashíd talking and Art was going to have to make the best of playing grand vizier. He wondered how many people knew Harún er Rashíd came out in English as Aaron the Just.

But the *Thousand Nights and a Night* dated from a smaller simpler world where every litigant could crouch in the courtyard for a day or

a week until the sultan tired of music, hunting, copulating, and
turned his jaded mind to justice. How the hell were they going to run
a planet?

Finally they were aboard the flagship again and when Art's stomach, already queasy from the funny grav of the shuttle, got over the
sudden assault of Arab cookery and camel dung he eventually realized he was hungry. He intended to remind Jorf about the stink but
the Old Man didn't seem to mind. There were more important things.

The Spanish pharmacist was munching a *tapa* made of a hard white
roll and paper-thin slices of *jamón serrano*.

"Where'd you get the ham?" Art asked.

The pharmacist fiddled with the synthesizer and handed Art a
sandwich to go with his *café con leche*. It tasted like the real thing.
The pharmacist must have spent days dorking about with this machine to re-create the pungent flavor of mountain ham. Art wished he
had never tasted Star's gourmet meal.

The Spaniard waited till Art had finished eating, then said, "Your
friend died."

It seemed to Art that he had never been more alone. "Where is
he?" he finally asked.

"Back where he came from."

Naturally. No use letting seventy kilos of perfectly good protein get
out of the eco system. He had first met Baz coming out of a recycling
tank. Now the old man was back in it—without a suit. Art wished he
could think of something profound and bitter to say but he only felt
drained. "What're you going to do when you go home?" he asked the
Spaniard.

"You think I want to go back?"

Art hadn't thought of it that way. He realized he didn't really want
to go back to Nebraska either. But he hadn't expected to spend the
rest of his life in space—not even aboard a planet-sized ship like the
Nishrub II. But after Jorf's *coup d'état* . . . That speech had burned
his last— He got to his feet and went to the bridge. Bercovici was just
entering too. "Can you put me through to Nebraska?"

Bercovivi nodded. *"Aqui o privato?"*

"In there I guess." Art went back where the pharmacist still sipped
café con leche.

"Hello." It was Pop's voice.

"Are they leaving you alone?"

"Oh hello, Art!" Pop gave a cackling laugh. "You sure put the fear of God into those crew-cut bastards. I s'pose they're still listening in but yeah, your mother'n I're gettin' along just fine."

"Do you need anything?"

There was a moment's silence. "If you mean what you said this morning nobody's ever gonna need anything."

"What'd you think of it?"

"Never knew you had it in you," Pop said. "Stick with it, kid. Especially that part about one hundred per cent inheritance tax."

"You really think that's fair?" Suddenly Art remembered he shouldn't be asking questions like this over an open line.

"Sure it's fair. Best thing anybody can give his children is a good body and a chance to earn a living. Now they'll all start out even without some millionaire buying a presidency just to keep his shithead son out of the pool hall."

Art guessed Pop and Mom really were all right now. "Do you think the big wheels'll go for it?"

"They like to live too."

Art exchanged pleasantries with Mom, who had been listening on the bedroom extension. The Spaniard was still fiddling with the hot drink synthesizer as she said, "Don't give up the ship," and hung up. "*¿Sus padres?*" he asked. Art had forgotten that he spoke no English.

A head poked through the doorway. "How'd it go?" Lafferty asked. Art was startled. "I should have taken you back down. I'm sorry."

"What for?" the newsman asked. "This is where the action is."

"Yeah."

"Cheer up, kid. Someday you can retire."

Art wondered what was wrong. What did he want? Nothing really. He had hoped all this terror and commotion would end someday and he could go back to that open sewer they called the Mediterranean. He made a mental note. Now that there was energy to spare those countries would have to stop dumping raw sewage—

Lafferty punched buttons and a moment later Walter Cronkite was exuding trustworthiness from the bulkhead. "—while most people wait to see how these programs will be reduced from rhetoric to practical application, one family has already made its decision." Fast cut to a familiar face speaking clipped Bostonian. "—turning over the bulk of the estate to the general fund. The family assumes the federal government will be handling this kind of thing until a world government can be formed. In any event, life has been good to us. Now it's time to practice what we've always preached." There was another cut back to a quizzical smile on the good gray Walter. "And that's the way it is," he said. "Good night."

And that's the way it was for over a year as Art played at Grand Vizier of Earth. After the first frantic rush past newly opened borders people began drifting back out of the cities, back where life was open and free. *Free was the operative word.*

Yet Art was daily surprised by how hard many people worked once they no longer had to. Jorf was visibly older, his graying bullet head nearly white. Art was exhausted. The dispensing of justice was turning out to be an endless treadmill of a job. How could two men possibly take care of every outrage perpetrated on the long-suffering people of Earth?

Art had not been back down since that momentous day at the UN. Slowly the *Nishrub II* was filling up with administrative personnel, many of them young and female, few averse to getting close to the seat of power. Yet Art missed Earth. Not Nebraska. He was homesick for a country where he had lived only a few months, most of them in hiding. There was something about Spain . . . there was also something about Number One. Art wondered if Jérstar had come unharmed out of the repair center the day after the sky had fallen. But mostly he wondered if he would ever have ten minutes to himself.

"*Ahtt!*"

"Sir!"

"Indonesia killing Chinese again."

Art sighed. Every once in a while something like this happened. Not nearly as often as he had expected though. It had taken a while for him to understand that Baz had been right: Alliance-THEM turkey shoots had been dual in their purpose. Not only did they drain off the aggressions of THEM planets. The battle had in one fell swoop killed nearly everybody on Earth who cared enough about fighting to volunteer.

Except one exceeding dangerous man. "Do we drop a bomb?" Art asked.

"No," Jorf said. "People got the ones did the killing. They want to know what to do with them. You still got room?"

There were several million humans asleep in the bowels of the *Nishrub II*. Soon Art knew they would have to face the problem of what to do with them. Jorf had promised that anyone who killed would be killed. He didn't know how not to violate his own decree.

So far the *Nishrub II* had not dropped a single bomb. The missiles were "clean" but the smallest would take out half a continent. Some people in South China had thought Jorf would not dare use them. Jorf had set up a computer analogue to predict how high the sea would rise if he were to bring the starship into stationary orbit over South China. The print-out had been sufficient.

"Ahtt, you think is better now?" Jorf sounded wistful.

Art didn't know. "We've never pressured the news media," he said. "But sometimes I wonder if it's as good as it all sounds up here."

In the year since Jorf had clotured the UN the birthrate had dropped. This had eased food and housing problems. Imperceptibly, food aboard the ship had improved too, though Art had been unaware of it until one day he sipped that same mind-blowing tea Star had fed him. So the others, cook and pharmacist at least, had also been exposed to the joys of Number One's food. The tea's ability to enhance any flavor had made Earth's limited varieties of food less monotonous. Meanwhile a few roads had been torn up and put back into agriculture. A few housing tracts had been relocated on barren hillside land and orange groves replanted.

THEM technology provided hydrogen and oxygen from water, so cheap that cars would have converted even if the new fuels had not been clean-burning. Improved hovercraft used oceans, rivers, even passed over fields without damaging crops, and eliminated offloading from ship to truck. Like most transport revolutions, the prime mover was not edict but efficiency.

But was life better? Art suspected that no matter how benevolent, many were less than ecstatic about life under a dictatorship.

"Maybe it's time for elections," Jorf mused.

Six months ago Art would have been overjoyed at the prospect of somebody else taking over this dirty and thankless job. He guessed he still was. "Shall I announce it?"

Jorf nodded.

"When?"

"Day after tomorrow."

"But that won't give any candidate time to—"

Jorf smiled. "They've had longer than we have."

Art hadn't thought of it that way.

Lafferty drifted in. The newsman had attached himself permanently to the *Nishrub II*. It was odd the way power drew hangers-on. Art had often wondered if Lafferty was as wholehearted in his support of Jorf as he seemed to be. "Going to be an election day after tomorrow," he said. "You want to break it?"

"Kind of short notice, isn't it?"

"Yes," Jorf said.

"I see. Any restrictions?"

"No. I want it run honest."

"Will you be a candidate?"

Jorf's face was expressionless. "I think I'll give a State of the Union message."

Lafferty laughed. Art wished uneasily that he knew what the newsman was laughing at.

Art had tried to get Jorf to plan his speeches, pointing out that the ship's interpreter-computer could do a better job, and do it instantaneously in every language. Still the Arab insisted on filtering every public utterance through Art.

"We got to go back down," Jorf said.

Lafferty raised his eyebrows.

"Why go down there and get shot at by some nut who wants a job I never wanted in the first place?" Art asked.

"What your captain means," Lafferty explained, "is all the other candidates are down there taking their chances. What'll it look like if you stay up here?"

Like common sense, Art wanted to say, but Jorf's hooded gaze made him instead ask, "With all the strangers we've brought aboard, and THEM still trotting around loose, what makes you think it's safe up here?"

"Not safe," Jorf agreed. "Not with three million losers stacked in those tanks. Some sorehead wakes them up . . ."

Art was consoled with the knowledge that he was not the only one who worried.

"That's why I speak from the UN," the Arab continued. "We go down right now before somebody has time to cook something up."

"Could you give me a rough idea what you're going to say?" Art asked. But Jorf was on his feet already.

All the way down Art worried. Jorf had never been a predictable man. The last year had taken its toll. There were times when Art suspected the Old Man wanted out even more than he.

They faced the General Assembly again, faces of every size, shape, and color. The thing they had in common was the look Shakespeare had once ascribed to Cassius. Wolves, as Art recalled, were relatively social animals. He tried to stand to one side but Jorf adroitly stepped back where Art could hear him but the microphone could not.

"Day after tomorrow you vote," Jorf said. "If you want, you vote me. If not, vote somebody else. You vote me, we gonna build another ship big as *Nishrub II*. Anybody wants, we go exploring."

Art rendered it in slightly more elegant English and waited for the next burst. Jorf was through. Before anyone realized his campaign speech was finished, they were in a chopper heading for the shuttle at Kennedy.

CHAPTER SEVENTEEN

To no one's great surprise, Jorf won. There was considerable surprise when, through Art, he assured the world that another election would be held six months from now in case anyone had second thoughts.

Lafferty was amused. "Pulled their teeth again," the newsman said. Art wasn't sure what he meant.

"All over Earth," Lafferty explained, "little men have been preparing big speeches about how he stole the election, didn't give them time to prepare and all that. Now, instead of bitching, they've got to come up with something better than he's offering."

"What would that be?" Art wondered.

"By the way," Lafferty continued, "they caught the Alliance ambassador."

"Where?"

"Madagascar, Malagasy—whatever they're calling it nowadays."

"Hiding?"

"Unfortunately they removed his hide while he was still alive."

Art sighed. He found it difficult to feel any compassion for the snake-oil salesman who caused all this but there were laws and now he was going to have to do something about it. "I thought he'd bugged out."

"He and the Alliance training officers made a touching speech about how their mission was ended and they were going off to spread the good word in another system, then they got into a shuttle and took off."

"You suppose they were heading for this ship?"

"Where else? The shuttle ran low on food and air. They had to put down somewhere."

"When'd they catch him?"

"About a month ago."

"Why didn't I hear about it?"

"Apparently the locals didn't want to put you to any unnecessary trouble."

Art wished he still didn't know about it. That was the trouble with this job. Everything was black and white until the first actual problem came up and the man in charge had to deal with living, breathing, bleeding human beings instead of abstractions. It was getting Jorf down. It was getting everybody down.

"I've also got some other news for you."

Art waited.

Lafferty glanced around the lounge. "Are we bugged?"

"Nobody's ever worked out all the circuitry on this ship. We could be broadcasting live to Earth for all I know."

Lafferty produced a tape player with a cassetteful of particularly noisy acid rock. Muttering through the boomings of a Fender bass, he said, "There are people who want you to take over."

Art reached past him and switched off the tape player. "I don't want to hear any more."

Lafferty turned it back on. "You'd better listen."

Art ran from the compartment. Straight into Jorf. "Something wrong?" the Arab asked.

"Not really." Art went to his own compartment and locked it. But he couldn't sleep. What, he wondered, was the big deal? People had tried to buy the blue-eyed shuttle pilot. Nearly every man of the original *Nishrub* crew had been approached at one time or another. It had been so common during the first months that they didn't even bother to report these attempts. But lately . . .

Art had thought things were getting better, that people were content with Jorf's benevolent rule. He remembered when people had slaved to support huge military machines, to buy good living for dictatorial bureaucracies. Did they really want to go back to wars, boundaries?

He remembered a conversation with Baz before the old alien had died. "The British Empire had fewer policemen per capita than any other in the history of your planet. When its components regained independence they immediately reverted to tribalism, blood feuds, and genocide. Did the common people really want to exchange the British Resident for a witch doctor? Or was the whole independence movement nothing but a few overeducated local scoundrels angling for a license to steal?"

Art tried to remember how he had felt before he had been sucked up into all this. Mostly he had just wanted to be free to wear his hair any way he chose, free to earn a living or starve. All his life he had yearned for one simple thing. That, he guessed, was why he missed Spain and not Nebraska. In Spain people had left him alone. Until he had nearly drowned and Jorf had saved his life. He wondered if ever again he could somehow arrange his life . . . couldn't they just leave him alone for a minute?

He twisted for the hundredth time, rubbed his eyes, and walked back to the bridge. Jorf was scanning a readout. "Something wrong?" he asked.

"I need a vacation."

"Take plenty of money."

"If I did it wouldn't be a vacation."

Jorf sighed and for an instant Art saw what it must have been like to be a poor Moroccan boy making the best of it while strangers looted his country. "You born poor, you always poor," the Arab said. "Where you go?"

"Spain, I think. Can you spare me for a month?"

"Sure. I'll use the machine for a Talker. Moonface can do other things."

"Moonface!"

Jorf grinned. "You don't trust him?"

"Well sure but—"

"He runs things a month, people be damn glad you come back."

"By the way," Art said. "I think it'd be wise if you got rid of Lafferty."

Jorf gave him a level look. "How would we keep in touch with them?"

Art stared back. Did Jorf really have a nictitating membrane? "You know what he's doing?"

"Didn't you?"

"I still don't."

"Next time you listen," Jorf said. "Meanwhile, go have a good time."

Dazedly, Art began packing. Then he realized if he wanted any peace he would have to change his appearance. To hell with packing. He caught a shuttle and rode down with a load of VIP sight-seers still euphoric from funny air, funny grav, and funny cocktails. Mostly they were speaking German. None recognized him.

It was encouraging. There was really nothing outstanding about his blond Scandinavian appearance. With luck he could evade the news noses and lose himself among the thousands of Swedes quietly berserking along the Costa del Sol. So many tourists, so many nationalities, surely nobody would remember him.

He had been in such a hurry that he hadn't even found out where this shuttle was landing. The VIPs were speaking German but the shuttle put down at Heathrow, which smelled of riverine damp and frying fish.

There were no "in transit" corrals or any of the customs and passport chicken guano that had plagued travelers for the last century. He was studying schedules to Spain when he realized that, though he had been to the asteroids, had seen life under another star, this was the first time he had ever been to London.

There was only one tube from the airport. The station seemed new. He wondered if the Piccadilly line would take him to Piccadilly Circus, wherever that was. An hour later he stood in the center of fogless, smogless London. It was nearing 11 P.M. local time and the streets were full. He stared at the offerings in play and movie houses, admired the local birds, and drifted into a pub. "Pint of bitter." He tried to sound British.

"Sorry, mate." The pubkeeper pointed at the clock.

Art had forgotten England's weird closing hours. "Where can I get a drink?"

The bartender studied his mixed Earth-THEM clothing. Tomorrow Art would have to see about suitable local color. "There are private clubs," the pubkeeper said. "Takes an honest face, good character references, and a pound note. You can get by without the first two but truth, mate, they're not worth it."

Art sighed and went out onto Shaftsbury again. Where was everyone going? By the time he found out every theater and pub in London had just closed. Every British subject and every tourist had just caught the last train. He waved for a cab. "What's the quickest way to Spain?"

"Have you considered boats or airplanes?" the cabbie asked. "Arfway to Dover and I'd be out of petrol."

Art wondered whatever happened to his alpenstock. He controlled himself and an hour later the cabbie had him in the Gatwick terminal waiting for a lumbering propellor-driven plane which was nonskedding several cars and their owners to Orly.

It was 0400 and raining when he landed outside Paris. With liberal applications of money and francophonic bullshit he was soon aboard a flight to Madrid. It was raining again when he got off the third flight from Madrid to Málaga. He wondered if he had been gilding his memories of the Costa del Sol. Come to think of it, it *had* rained quite a bit while he was there.

The taxi from the airport to downtown Málaga sagged from the liquid hydrogen conversion even before he and two burly Mitteleuropa types with briefcases and Hitler mustaches crowded in. At first they spoke German, then with a sidelong glance at Art slipped into Schweizerdeitsch. Art was too exhausted and discouraged to bother trying to understand. Taking a vacation didn't seem such a hot idea after all. He hoped he would feel better once he had gotten a night's sleep. Then, maybe after a breakfast of *café con leche* and *churros* in that place across from the fish market . . . He closed his eyes.

When he opened them again the taxi was groaning around switchback curves in brilliant sunlight. As it rounded a curve he saw Málaga below and behind. This had to be the road up through the mountains to Antequera and Sevilla. "What the hell's going on?"

"Did you sleep well, Mr. Jansen?"

"Oh, horseshit!" Art ran hands through his hair. He wasn't really frightened. Nobody would dare harm him unless they had a starship and another planet ready. "When I'm finished with my vacation," he said, "I'll be more inclined to entertain the proposals of those who respected my privacy."

"We've tried to approach you before," one said. "Through legitimate channels, then any way we could."

"I don't want to hear it. Not from you, not from Lafferty."

"Hopeless," one man said. "He believes his own propaganda."

"I've heard you study history," the other said. "Are you familiar with Alexander and his Companions?"

"Slightly," Art said.

"And are you familiar with the next two or three centuries of Diadochi?"

"What are you getting at?"

"He's not a student." The first man sighed and resettled his briefcase on his lap. "You mean well with such intensity that it never occurs to you that others also know they and their children have to live on Earth."

"What's wrong with the present setup?" Art asked.

"It's probably the best Earth has ever known. People felt the same while Alexander was alive. Then he died and the Diadochi started carving things up."

"We had our Kaiser," the other said. "Human and thus imperfect. Was Hitler better?"

"Get to the point."

"Your captain grows old."

"In Rome," Art said, "a soothsayer who predicted the Emperor's death made swift acquaintance with his own."

"We're not setting a date. But all men die. When he does, what happens?"

"I'm sure somebody will be willing to tackle the job."

"But not you?"

"Do I look power hungry?"

"No."

Art wondered why the man seemed disappointed. "You may not think much of my captain's intellectual attainments," Art said. "I don't think much of them myself. But when times were bad he took care of me—of all of us. If you think I'd do anything behind his back then you'd probably believe I haven't been transmitting since the moment I woke up."

"We know."

Art ran his hands through his hair again.

"Don't worry. It's working. We too have nothing to hide."

"Then what the hell do you want?"

"We want you to give some thought to your successor."

"You're talking to the wrong man," Art said. "I'm not in line for anything."

The toothbrushed men looked at each other. "He really believes it!" one marveled.

"I suppose you have one all picked out for me?" Art asked.

"No, Mr. Jansen. You must pick your own." The taxi came to a wide spot in the winding road and turned back downhill toward Málaga.

All the way down the toothbrush-mustached pair conversed in Schweizerdeitsch. This time Art paid attention but the Swiss have for centuries practiced the art of obfuscation until their mountain dialect is unintelligible. He wondered if that was why they were so roundly despised by Germans and Austrians. Perhaps it was the other way around.

The taxi stopped before the statue of ibn-Gabirol in the little park below the Alcazaba. "Thank you for your time, Mr. Jansen," one of the men said. "We hope you enjoy your holiday."

"If anything happens to my captain—" Art promised.

"Exactly. We wish you both a long and happy life." The taxi drove down toward the waterfront and disappeared around a corner. Art found a bar full of German and American tourists. He went in and ordered *café con leche*.

"Jorf," he muttered, "are you there, can you hear me?"

There was no answer. His coffee didn't seem as good as he remembered. He went looking for a cheap room.

And once more something was wrong. Art was willing to swear nobody had recognized him or followed him but when he wandered past the new market toward the square where Picasso had been born and finally found an *alojamiento* the landlady was too young, too attractive, and, for a Spanish girl, several thousand per cent too friendly. He wondered if the whorehouse district had moved. It was nearing siesta time. He took the room and flopped without even removing his shoes.

Several hours later he woke refreshed but with no more understanding than before. He ran his hand through his hair again. Odds and ends from the ship came through faintly. Maybe the Earth had turned a little since . . . That made no sense. There were repeater satellites everywhere. "Jorf," he asked, "can you hear me?"

"Yah, Ahtt. Something wrong?"

"I don't know. Everything okay up there?"

"Everything fine. You having good time?"

"No. Did you hear what happened?"

"Where?"

"With me a few hours ago."

"I can't listen to everything."

"When you get time, have somebody play back the monitors. Maybe you can figure out what they want."

"Hokay," Jorf said. "You have good time." Which left Art as confused as ever. He wondered how long it would take for Jorf to contact him.

It was cool on the beach, with a gritty wind that stiffened the follicles of the hardiest Scandinavian. Art strolled morosely, kicking sand from between his toes. After so long off Earth his feet did not take kindly to sandals or sand. He found himself comparing these lissome blondes with the violet-haired jérs of Number One. What did those two Hitler-mustached types want? Nothing they had said made sense. They wouldn't dare harm him. They couldn't reach Jorf . . .

"*Ahtt!*"

"Yeah!" A blonde in a less-than-nothing bikini glanced up from her book with a smile ready, then saw he was not looking at her. "Where can I catch a shuttle?" Art asked. "I've had enough vacation."

"Where you? Málaga?"

"Yeah."

All the way back up Art wondered if the Arab had really had Moonface running his affairs. He wondered how long it would take him to get things back to an acceptable level of chaos.

Leaving the shuttle, he couldn't decide whether the diesel-fish stink of Earth was worse than cooking and camel dung. The watch on the bridge were all new. He wandered to the galley and saw—Moonface. The singer of obscene songs smiled widely. "Have you really been running things while I was gone?" Art asked.

Moonface smiled again and offered tea. Art guessed Jorf had been having his little joke. "You're not a plant, are you?" he said in English. Moonface smiled. "Life," Art sighed, "would be so much simpler if we all had fairy godfathers or totem animals or whatever." Abruptly he saw that Moonface was eating the same spartan gruel they had always eaten aboard the *Nishrub*.

"Didn't anybody ever clue you in on the good stuff?" Art felt sudden sadness at the way this well-meaning dimwit had been left out. He got to his feet and punched a proper meal. He put the tray before Moonface.

The singer of obscene songs smiled and shook his head.

"Tastes good," Art said.

Moonface put a hand over his crotch.

Sonofabitch! This man is going to father a child and I'm not! Art tried not to show his consternation. No matter how they planned and rigged, humanity was going to outwit any engenic scheme. Succession . . . was this what those toothbrush-mustache types had been getting at? No way! Art forced a smile and patted Moonface on the shoulder.

Jorf wandered in and found a tray.

"We've got to do something about the stink on this ship," Art said.

"What stink?" the Arab asked. "By the way, you seen the new ship?"

That was something else Art had been wanting to ask about. "Couldn't we use that money better on Earth?"

Jorf didn't give him the usual level look. His smile was sad as he waved at Bercovici. The engineer nodded and they went into a debugged room.

"You ready?" Jorf asked.

"For what?"

"To take over."

Art stared. "Did you listen to those tapes?"

Jorf nodded.

"I don't *want* to take over," Art said. "If you believe that, why'd you ever let me come back up here?"

"You think *I* want?"

Art stared.

"You good boy," Jorf said. "You don't like to be king. Maybe you be good king because you don't like."

"Are you sick?"

"Sick hell! I feel fine. Couple of months we go."

"Where are we going?"

"You and *Nishrub II* stay here. You got to run Earth."

"But what about you?"

"The new ship," Jorf explained. "Somebody gotta be captain. Good job for me."

"But what about me—what about Earth?"

"You learn. Just don't ever believe your own bullshit. Besides, going to be easier when I go."

"Easier? You're the guy who's held it all together. Those sons of bitches'll eat me alive!"

"No," Jorf promised. "Sons of bitches all going with me. Anybody don't like to live nice and quiet going to enlist and go out with me. Plenty fighting, plenty loot, every month a nice rape."

Art didn't want to believe it but he remembered Baz. It made a horribly logical kind of sense. What kind of people always made up the first wave? Spanish and Portuguese freebooters had opened up the Americas. Now Earth's undesirables were going to bring civilization to some other unsuspecting planet. Win or lose, the undesirables would be bled off and another planet would be that much closer to civilization. *I called Baz cruel, his wife unfeeling. What will somebody call me?*

"You good boy," Jorf said. "You gonna do all right."

Art sighed. He wished now that he'd taken that vacation.